NEVER BEFORE HAS
A CONTEST HELD
SO MUCH PROMISE –
OR SO MUCH DANGER.

ONE FALSE NOTE

THE 39 CLUES

GORDON KORMAN

SCHOLASTIC INC.

NEW YORK TORONTO LONDON AUCKLAND SYDNEY
MEXICO CITY NEW DELHI HONG KONG BUENOS AIRES

For all the brother-sister teams,
from the Mozarts through the Cahills,
from a grateful only child
— GK

Library of Congress Control Number: 2008926487

ISBN-13: 978-0-545-06042-4
ISBN-10: 0-545-06042-7

10 9 8 7 6 5 4 3 2 1   08 09 10 11 12

Book design and illustration by SJI Associates, Inc.
Book cover photos of Dan and Amy by James Levin © Scholastic Inc.
Image of Marie Antoinette courtesy of the Bridgeman Art Library/Getty Images

First edition, December 2008

Printed in China

Scholastic US: 557 Broadway • New York, NY 10012
Scholastic Canada: 604 King Street West • Toronto, ON M5V 1E1
Scholastic New Zealand Limited: Private Bag 94407 • Greenmount, Manukau 2141
Scholastic UK Ltd.: Euston House • 24 Eversholt Street • London NW1 1DB

CHAPTER 1

The hunger strike began two hours east of Paris.

Saladin took a single dainty whiff of the open cat food tin and turned up his nose.

"Come on, Saladin," coaxed fourteen-year-old Amy Cahill. "Here's your dinner. It's a long way to Vienna."

The Egyptian Mau emitted a haughty snort that was a clinic in nonverbal communication: *You've got to be kidding me.*

"He's used to red snapper," Amy said apologetically to Nellie Gomez, the Cahills' au pair.

Nellie was unmoved. "Do you have any idea how much fresh fish costs? We've got to make our money last. Who knows how long we'll be running around looking for these precious clues of yours?"

Saladin let out a disapproving *"Mrrp!"*

Dan Cahill, Amy's eleven-year-old brother, looked up from the page of sheet music he was examining. "I'm with you, dude. I can't believe we had to take the slowest train in Europe. We've got to get *moving!*

The competition has private jets, and we're wasting time on the Loser Express. Are we going to stop in every podunk town in France?"

"No," Nellie told him honestly. "Pretty soon it'll stop in every podunk town in Germany. Then every podunk town in Austria. Look, it was cheap, okay? I didn't agree to babysit you guys on this quest—"

"Au pair us on the quest," Dan amended.

"—just to have you drop out halfway through because you blew all your cash on snapper and expensive train tickets," she concluded.

"We really appreciate your help, Nellie," Amy told her. "We could never do this without you."

Amy was still dizzy from the whirlwind of the past two weeks. *One minute you're an orphan; the next, you're part of the most powerful family the world has ever known!*

An unbelievable twist for two kids who had been palmed off on an uncaring guardian who, in turn, palmed them off on a series of au pairs. Now they knew the truth—they were relatives of Benjamin Franklin, Wolfgang Amadeus Mozart, and more—geniuses, visionaries, and global leaders.

We were nobody. Suddenly we have a chance to shape the world. . . .

All thanks to the contest their grandmother Grace had set up in her will. Somehow, the secret of the Cahills' centuries-old power had been lost—a secret that could only be found by assembling 39 Clues. Those

Clues were hidden all around the globe. So this was a treasure hunt. But *what* a treasure hunt—spanning oceans and continents, with nothing less than world domination as the prize.

Yet high stakes meant high risks. Their rivals would stop at nothing to defeat them. Already there had been casualties.

There will probably be many more. . . .

Amy regarded Dan in the seat opposite her. *Two weeks ago, we were fighting over the TV remote. . . .*

She couldn't seem to get through to Dan how weird it all was. Her brother saw nothing unusual about belonging to the strongest, most influential family in history. He accepted it without question. After all, it said great things about *him*. He saw no drawbacks to being a high roller in the scheme of things. The poor kid was only eleven—no parents, and now even Grace was gone.

In all the excitement over the contest, they had hardly mourned their grandmother's death. It didn't seem right. Amy and Grace Cahill had been so close. Still, Grace was the one who had started them on this dangerous roller coaster. Sometimes Amy didn't know what to feel. . . .

She shook her head to clear it and focused on her brother. He was scouring the sheet music, looking for hidden markings or secret writing.

"Any luck?" Amy asked him.

"Zilch," he told her. "Are you sure this Mozart dude was a Cahill? I mean, Ben Franklin hardly blew his nose without planting a coded message in the Kleenex. This is nothing but boring music."

Amy rolled her green eyes. " 'This Mozart dude'? Were you born a dweeb, or did you have to get a diploma? Wolfgang Amadeus Mozart is considered the greatest classical composer who ever lived."

"Right, classical. Boring."

"Musical notes correspond to the letters A through G," Nellie mused. "Maybe there's a message that way."

"Been there, done that," Dan reported. "I even tried unscrambling the letters in case the words were ana-grams. Face it — we almost got killed for a clue that isn't really a clue."

"It's a clue," Amy insisted. "It has to be."

Clues. 39 of them. Never before had a contest held so much promise — or so much danger. With ultimate power hanging in the balance, the deaths of two American orphans would be barely a footnote.

But we didn't die. We found the first clue — after a treacherous obstacle course through the life of Benjamin Franklin. Amy was convinced that Mozart was the key to the second. The answer lay at the end of these railroad tracks in Vienna, where Mozart had lived and composed some of the greatest music of all time.

They could only hope that the competition wouldn't get there first.

"I hate France," muttered Hamilton Holt, clutching a tiny hamburger in his massive hand. "It's like the whole country's on a diet."

The Holts stood at the lunch counter in the small railroad station thirty kilometers east of Dijon, France. They hoped to pass for an American family on vacation, but they looked more like the offensive line of a football team — even the twin daughters, who were no older than Dan.

"Eyes on the prize, Ham," Eisenhower Holt reminded his son. "When we find the thirty-nine clues, we can kiss these starvation rations good-bye and hit some all-you-can-eat buffets back in the States. But for now, we've got to catch up with those Cahill brats."

Madison took a bite of her own lunch and made a face. "There's too much mustard!"

"It's Dijon, stupid," her twin, Reagan, told her. "This is the mustard capital of the world."

Madison sucker punched her in the stomach. The blow would have stopped a rhino in its tracks, but Reagan just stuck her tongue out defiantly. It took a lot to damage a Holt.

"Quiet, girls," Mary-Todd, their mother, admonished fondly. "I think I hear the train."

The family watched as the ancient diesel engine lumbered into view.

Madison frowned. "I thought trains in Europe were supposed to be fast."

"They're tricky, those Cahills, just like their parents," her father replied. "They took the last train we'd ever suspect to find them on. Okay, formation."

The family was used to Eisenhower's coaching lingo. He might have been kicked out of West Point, but that didn't mean he wasn't a great motivator. And nothing motivated the Holts like a chance to get even with their uppity relatives. This contest was the chance to prove they were as Cahill as any of them. They would be the first to find the 39 Clues—even if they had to chop all the others into coleslaw to make it happen.

They scattered, disappearing into the woods beyond the station.

The slow train chugged to a halt at the platform, and a few passengers disembarked. The conductors and station porters were too busy unloading luggage to notice the burly family of five climbing into the rear car. The Holts were aboard.

They began to search the coaches, working their way forward. The plan was to avoid attention, but that wasn't easy for the king-size Holts. Shoulders and knees were jostled. Feet were stepped on. Dirty looks were exchanged, along with mumbled curses in several different languages.

In the third car, Hamilton's swinging elbow knocked a woman's hat off, causing her to drop the birdcage in her lap. The carrier clattered to the floor, the startled parakeet inside chirping and flapping its wings in agitation. Six rows ahead, this brought Saladin scrambling up the seat back to investigate. And when Amy looked to see what was bothering the cat—

"The Ho-Ho-" Moments of stress always brought out her stammer.

"Holts," Dan breathed in alarm.

Luckily, the parakeet owner stooped to rescue the cage, blocking the aisle. Dan quickly shut Saladin and the sheet music into the overhead luggage bin.

"Come on, lady—" Eisenhower grumbled impatiently. Then he spotted Dan.

The big man plowed right over parakeet and owner. Dan grabbed Amy by the hand and fled for the opposite end of the car.

Nellie kicked a backpack into the aisle in front of Eisenhower's running feet, and he belly flopped to the floor.

"*Excusez-moi, monsieur,*" Nellie said in perfect French, reaching to help him up.

Eisenhower batted her hand away. Out of options, she sat on him, pressing her full weight between his shoulder blades.

"What are you doing, you crazy foreigner?"

"That's no foreigner, Dad!" Hamilton effortlessly plucked the au pair off his father and tossed her into her seat. "It's the Cahill brats' nanny!"

"I'll scream," Nellie threatened.

"Then I'll throw you through the window of the train," Hamilton promised. He spoke so matter-of-factly that there was little doubt he was both willing and able to do exactly that.

Eisenhower scrambled to his feet. "Keep her on ice, Ham. Don't take your eyes off her for a second."

He charged away, leading the stampede of Holts, predators in pursuit of prey.

Amy and Dan had already made it through the connector to the restaurant car. They raced between diners, dodging steaming plates of food. Dan risked a backward glance. The enraged features of Eisenhower Holt filled the window of the pass-through.

He nudged a waiter and pointed. "See that guy? He says you put steroids in his soup!"

Amy grabbed her brother's arm and fixed him with fearful eyes, hissing, "How can you joke about this? You know how dangerous they are!"

The Cahills scrambled through the hatch and burst into the next car. "Tell me about it," Dan said nervously. "I wish I could fit into a luggage bin like Saladin. Don't they have security on this train? Surely France has a law against five Neanderthals picking on a couple of kids."

Amy was horrified. "We can't talk to security! We can't risk anybody asking questions about who we are and what we're doing. Remember, Social Services is still looking for us in Boston." She threw open the door of the forward pass-through and pushed Dan in ahead of her.

It was the mail car. Hundreds of canvas bags were piled everywhere, along with packages and crates of all shapes and sizes.

"Amy—" Dan began to stack boxes in front of the hatch.

His sister understood instantly. They worked together to build a barricade of parcels, wedging the topmost—a freeze-dried ham—under the door handle. Dan tried the lever. It didn't budge.

A flurry of shouts came from the adjoining car. The Holts were almost upon them.

Amy and Dan made a break for the forward passage, dodging mailbags. Amy stepped into the connector and reached for the hatch to the next coach.

Locked.

She pounded on the scratched glass. Beyond it was a crew lounge, with couches and cots, all empty. She banged harder. No response.

They were cornered.

Across the car, Eisenhower's granite face appeared in the window. The whole train seemed to shake as he slammed his shoulder against the door.

"They're our cousins," Amy reasoned uncertainly. "They'd never *really* hurt us . . ."

"They almost left us buried alive in Paris!" Dan shot back. From the floor he pulled up a hockey stick wrapped in brown paper.

"You can't be serious . . . !"

At that moment, Eisenhower Holt took a running leap at the door. With a teeth-jarring crash, the hatch splintered loose and slammed into Dan. The boy went down hard. The stick clattered to the floor.

"Dan!" Blinded by rage, Amy snatched the stick and broke it over Eisenhower's head. The big man absorbed the blow, wobbled, and collapsed on a mailbag.

Dan sat up, amazed. "Whoa! Knockout!"

The victory was short-lived. Holts stormed the car.

Madison grabbed Amy by the collar. Reagan yanked Dan upright.

They were caught.

CHAPTER 2

"Sugar maple!" Mary-Todd Holt knelt over her husband. "Are you all right?"

Eisenhower sat up, an egg-size lump blooming on his crown. "Of course I'm all right!" he managed, his words slurred. "You think a little insect can stop *me*?"

Reagan was unconvinced. "I don't know, Dad. She brained you with a baseball bat!"

"Hockey stick," Dan corrected.

"Those could be your last words, brat —" The victim leaped to his feet, then reeled and almost went down again.

His wife reached out to steady him, but Eisenhower shook her off. "I'm fine. It's just the motion of the train. You think I can't take a shot? They said that at the Point, and look at me now!"

"What do you want?" Amy demanded.

"*That's* putting on your thinking cap," Mary-Todd approved. "Give us the clue from Paris, and nothing will happen to you."

"It's better than you deserve," her husband added, rubbing his head gingerly.

"We don't have it," Amy told them. "The Kabras took it."

"They took the *bottle*," Madison corrected. "Don't worry, they'll pay soon enough. You've got the paper."

"What paper?" Dan asked defiantly.

In reply, Eisenhower grasped Dan by the collar and lifted him as easily as he might have raised his arm to signal a waiter. "Listen, you little stinkbug. You think you're hot stuff because you two were Grace's favorites. But to me, the pair of you mean less than what gets cleaned out of the bottom of a birdcage!"

His massive paw closed on Dan's neck, squeezing like an industrial-strength vise. Dan gasped for breath and realized he had none. He was being strangled.

His eyes sought his sister's, but he found no help there, only a mirror image of his own horror. It was easy to laugh at the Holts, with their bodybuilder physiques, their gung ho coaching jargon, and their matching warm-up suits. This was the chilling wake-up call. They were dangerous enemies. And with the stakes so high, they were capable of —

Of what?

Amy wasn't willing to find out. "Stop it! We'll give you anything you want!"

Madison was triumphant. "I told you they'd fold under the full-court press."

"Now, Madison," her mother admonished. "Amy did the smart thing. Not all Cahills have what it takes."

Amy ran to help Dan, who had been dropped unceremoniously onto a lumpy mailbag. With relief, she noted that normal color was returning to his cheeks.

He was upset. "You shouldn't have done that!"

"Grace wouldn't want us to get killed," she whispered. "We'll find another way."

The Holts began marching them toward the back of the train.

"Don't get any ideas," Eisenhower muttered as a porter sidled past them.

Reluctantly, they approached their seats. Hamilton sat with Nellie, his bodybuilder bulk pressing her painfully against the train window.

But the au pair's discomfort was instantly forgotten at the sight of Amy and Dan. "Did they hurt you?" she asked anxiously. "Are you all right?"

"We're fine," Amy said glumly. To Eisenhower, she added, "It's in the overhead."

The Holts very nearly trampled one another in their eagerness to get the luggage bin open. With a yowl, Saladin dropped to the floor. In his wake fluttered a blizzard of shredded paper — all that remained of the original sheet music penned by Mozart himself.

"Our clue!" Nellie wailed.

"*Your* clue?" The roar that came from Eisenhower was barely human. He grabbed Saladin, held him upside down, and shook him.

With a feline gulp that sounded more like a hic-cup, Saladin burped up a hairball liberally sprinkled with musical notes. There was nothing that could be salvaged. It was confetti.

Eisenhower Holt's explosion of temper proved that his muscles extended all the way to his vocal cords. The outburst sent passengers scurrying for adjoining cars. A moment later, a uniformed conductor rushed up the aisle, picking his way through the agitated travelers.

"What is going on here?" demanded the man in a heavy French accent. "You will show me your ticket for this train."

"You call this a train?" roared Eisenhower. "If this was back in the States, I wouldn't let my gerbil ride this rattletrap!"

The conductor flushed red. "You will surrender your passport, *monsieur*! At the next station, you will talk to the authorities!"

"Why wait?" Eisenhower thrust the cat into Amy's hands. "Take your rat. Holts—fast break!"

All five members of the family raced out the con-necting door and hurled themselves from the moving train.

Amy and Dan stared out the window at the sight of their cousins rolling down the hillside in tight formation.

"Wow!" Nellie breathed. "That's something you don't see every day."

Amy was close to tears. "I hate them! Now we've lost our only lead!"

"It wasn't much of a lead, Amy," Dan said softly. "Just music. Even if it was by Mozart—big whoop."

"It *is* a big whoop," his sister lamented. "Just because we couldn't find what was hidden in the piece doesn't mean it wasn't there. At least I wanted to play the notes on a piano. Maybe it would have told us something."

Her brother looked surprised. "You want the notes? That's easy enough." He folded down a tray table, opened a fresh napkin, and began to work.

Amy watched in amazement as he drew the five-line staff and began to place notes on it.

"You can't write music!"

"Maybe not," he agreed without looking up. "But I've been staring at that sheet since Paris. This is it. I guarantee it."

Amy didn't argue. Her brother had a photographic memory. Their grandmother had commented on it many times. Had she known back then that his talent would be of vital importance one day?

By the time the train rattled over the border into Germany, Dan had reproduced the sheet music, perfect in every detail.

Saladin was not allowed anywhere near it.

As Amy, Dan, and Nellie walked out of Vienna's Westbahnhof railway station, they had no way of knowing that they were being spied on.

In the backseat of a sleek black limousine parked opposite the main entrance, Natalie Kabra peered through high-powered binoculars, watching their every move.

"I see them," she said to her brother, Ian, seated beside her in the supple leather of the car's interior. She made a face. "They always look like homeless people. And where's their luggage? A duffel bag and backpacks. Are they really that poor?"

"Poor excuses for Cahills," Ian replied absently, contemplating a chess move on the limo's pull-down screen. Since Paris, he had been matching wits with a Russian supercomputer outside Vladivostok. "What a stupid move," he murmured to his opponent. "I thought computers were supposed to be smart."

Natalie was annoyed. "Ian, could you pay attention, please! Superior intelligence doesn't mean we can't still make a mess of this." Her brother was brilliant, but no one was as brilliant as Ian thought he was. Sometimes common sense was more valuable than IQ points. He had plenty of the latter. Natalie knew it was her job to add a touch of the former. She respected her brother's talents — but he had to be watched.

Chortling, Ian sacrificed a bishop, expertly plotting toward checkmate seven moves away. "*We* have the bottle from Paris," he reminded his sister. "None of the other teams stand a chance. Especially not those Cahill charity cases. The contest is ours to win."

"Or lose, if we get overconfident," his sister reminded him. "Wait — they're getting into a taxi." She tapped on the glass partition. "Driver — follow that car."

CHAPTER 3

When it came to hotels, bigger didn't always mean better — but their room at the Franz Josef was barely a closet. On the other hand, it was affordable, and Nellie pronounced it clean.

"I still say we should have stayed at the Hotel Wiener," Dan complained.

"It's pronounced *Vee-ner*," Nellie corrected. "And it means anyone who lives in Vienna — like Bostonians are from Boston."

"It's still funny," Dan insisted. "I'm going to go over there and see if I can get one of their signs for my collection."

"We don't have time for that," Amy barked, setting Saladin down. The cat immediately began exploring the room, as if he thought there might be fresh snapper hidden somewhere. "We made it to Vienna, but we still have no idea what to do."

Dan unzipped Nellie's duffel and removed his laptop computer. "You can stare at musical notes until your eyes bug out," he said, plugging in the 220 adapter and powering up. "If the answer's anywhere, it's online."

Amy was disgusted. "You think you can Google the solution to all the world's problems."

"No, but I can Google Mozart." His eyes widened. "Wow — thirty-six million hits! Look at this one — *Mozart, the most famous Wiener of all time.* I'll bet the Oscar Mayer people would give them an argument about that."

"I'm pretty sure it's my job to tell you to grow up," Nellie said absently, gazing out the window. "You know, Vienna is a really beautiful city. Look at the architecture — I'll bet some of those buildings date back to the thirteenth century!"

Amy pointed. "I think that's the tower of St. Stephen's cathedral. It must be as tall as an office building back in the US!"

Everywhere, gargoyles and elaborate carvings decorated stone facades, and gold leaf accents gleamed in the sunlight. Beyond the nearest rooftops, a wide boulevard, the Ringstrasse, carried traffic and pedestrians to and fro.

Dan noticed none of this, entirely focused on his web surfing. "Look, Amy. I copied all that dumb music over for nothing. The whole thing's on the Internet. What was that piece called again?"

Amy rushed to his side and peered over his shoulder. "KV 617 — it was one of the last things Mozart wrote before he died . . . there it is!"

Dan scanned the sheet music, his brow furrowing. "Yeah, this is it—sort of. It's the same until here—" He pointed. "But then—"

Amy took out the napkin from the train and held it next to the screen. "It's different?"

"Not really," Dan mused. "See? It starts up again over here. But these three lines are missing from the Internet version. Weird, huh? It's almost like the website left something out."

"Or," breathed Amy, eyes dancing, "Mozart added three lines to the music he sent Ben Franklin in Paris! Dan—we could be looking at a secret message between two of the most famous people in history! These extra lines *are* the clue!"

Dan was unimpressed. "What difference does that make? We still don't know what it's supposed to mean."

Amy sighed anxiously. Her brother was immature and annoying. But perhaps his most unpleasant feature was the fact that he was usually right.

Mozarthaus, at Domgasse 5, was a museum/library dedicated to the famous composer. Located in Mozart's only preserved Vienna home, it was a popular tourist attraction. Even at nine o'clock in the morning, visitors were queued up halfway down the block, waiting to get in.

Dan was dismayed. "It's Mozart, not Disneyland! What are all these people doing here?"

His sister rolled her eyes. "This is the actual apartment Mozart lived in. Maybe even the bed where he slept. The chair he sat in. The inkwell he used to write some of the greatest music ever composed."

Dan made a face. "I'm standing in line to see a house full of old furniture?"

"Yes, you are," she said firmly. "Until we understand the meaning of that clue, our job is to learn as much about Mozart as we possibly can. Who knows when we'll see something that might tell us what we're looking for?"

"In a chair?" Dan said dubiously.

"Maybe. Look — we know the Holts are on our trail, and I'll bet the rest of the competition can't be too far behind them. They're older than us, smarter than us, and richer than us. We can't let up for a second."

It took forty minutes before they actually made it inside the door. Dan hadn't appreciated the wait, but now he was ready to admit that it had been the most interesting part of the tour.

Shoulder to shoulder with obnoxious sightseers and fawning music lovers, they shuffled through the great composer's apartment, following a trail of velvet ropes. One Australian tourist became so emotional in the presence of the Maestro that he actually wept.

"Don't cry, buddy. It'll be over soon," Dan murmured under his breath. Now if he could only make *himself* believe it.

The Cahill kids were told not to touch anything in at least six different languages. Every security guard in the building took one look at Dan and immediately knew he was capable of trashing the place.

With every *ooh* and *aah* from the Mozart-loving crowd, Dan's shoulders sagged a little lower. Amy was just as miserable, but for a different reason. Not knowing what you were looking for made a search all but impossible. She examined every expanse of white wall for coded markings until her head pounded and her eyes threatened to pop out of their sockets. But it soon became apparent that Mozarthaus was exactly what it seemed—a two-hundred-plus-year-old apartment that had been turned into a museum.

What did we expect to find? she reflected glumly. *A neon sign—Attention Cahills: Clue behind mirror?* Nothing in life came that easily.

As they headed for the exit, Dan emitted a loud exhalation of relief. "Thank God that's over. At least Ben Franklin had some cool inventions. This guy sat around all day writing music. Let's get out of here. I need to breathe some nonboring air."

Amy nodded reluctantly. There was nothing to be gained in this place. "I guess we should go back to the hotel. I wonder if Nellie managed to get Saladin to eat anything."

Dan looked concerned. "I think we might have to sell some of Grace's jewelry so we can afford snapper again."

All at once, Amy let out a little gasp and grabbed his arm.

"Okay, fine," Dan began. "Keep her necklace—"

"No, look. There's a library in the basement! A Mozart library!"

"Amy, don't do this to me! The antidote for boring isn't to find something even boringer!"

But when she went down the stairs and entered the gloomy, dusty library, he was at her side. After all, some of their best leads so far had come from libraries. And besides, if they left the Mozarthaus now empty-handed, it would mean he had suffered for nothing.

It wasn't a lending library. A single twenty-year-old computer held a list of library materials. Once you decided on what you wanted, you filled out a request and handed it to a librarian who looked like she could have been Mozart's grandmother.

They waited their turn at the terminal, and Amy took over the keyboard. She switched the language from German to English and searched first for KV 617 and then for Ben Franklin. Finding nothing they didn't already know, she shifted her focus to Mozart's personal life. That was where she discovered Maria Anna "Nannerl" Mozart.

"Mozart had an older sister!" she whispered shrilly.

"He has my sympathy," yawned Dan.

"I remember Grace mentioning her," Amy went on. "She was just as talented as Mozart, but she never got the training or the exposure because she was a girl."

She scrolled down. "And *look*! Her original diary is right in this library!"

Dan was miffed. He knew Amy had been closer with their grandmother, but even so, he didn't appreciate the reminder of how much the two had shared. "I thought we were looking for Mozart, not his sister."

"If Mozart was a Cahill, so was Nannerl," Amy pointed out. "But there's something else, too. Look at the two of us. This whole morning was a blur to you, and I remember every detail. What if it was the same with Mozart and Nannerl?"

"Great. Now you're calling Mozart stupid." He looked up in outrage. "And *me*!"

"Not stupid. But boys' brains are wired differently. I'll bet there are things Nannerl put in her journal that Wolfgang wouldn't have noticed in a million years."

She quickly scribbled a request form and handed it to the elderly librarian.

The woman regarded them with surprise. "This is a handwritten diary in the German language. Do you children read German?"

"W-well—" Amy began, flustered.

"We really need to see it," Dan piped up firmly. When the woman shuffled off in search of the volume, he whispered, "There must be something we can understand—maybe a drawing, or hidden notes, like on Franklin's stuff."

Amy nodded. Even the slightest hint was better than progress point zero.

They waited for what seemed like a long time. Then they heard a gasp and a little cry, and the librarian came running back, her face pale, her eyes wide. With trembling hands, she dialed the telephone and began speaking in a frantic voice. They could not understand her German, but Amy and Dan were able to make out a single ominous word — *polizei*.

"That means police!" Amy whispered urgently.

"Do you think she somehow found out we're wanted by Social Services back in Massachusetts?" Dan asked in dismay.

"How could she? We didn't even tell her our names!"

The answer came from the distraught librarian herself. "I am so sorry! This is a terrible tragedy! Nannerl's diary is missing! It has been stolen!"

CHAPTER 4

Nellie Gomez had never been a cat person. And that was before she'd become chief caregiver to an Egyptian Mau on a food-free diet. She switched off her iPod and regarded Saladin with concern. She had expected that the cat would be eating by now. But apparently, Saladin was tougher than he looked. She'd heard stories of Grace Cahill's monumental strength of character. Obviously, Amy and Dan's grandmother had managed to instill that trait in her pet.

Even more worrisome, Saladin was scratching compulsively around his neck and ears. She picked him up. "What's the matter, sweetie? Have you got fleas?"

She thought about fleas for a second and put the cat down swiftly. Nellie was game to put college on hold and take two kids on an around-the-world high-stakes treasure hunt. But she didn't do bugs.

There was the sound of a key in the lock, and Amy and Dan came in, feet dragging.

"Uh-oh," said Nellie. "Rough morning?"

"Oh, it was a blast," Dan replied sarcastically. "Picture a million-year-old house with no video games, and when you finally find a book to look at, it's not even there. What a bunch of idiots! They practically called out the army because of a diary that was probably eaten by termites a century ago."

"Termites eat wood, not paper," Amy reminded him, too tired and discouraged to work up a good argument. She hefted a bag. "Anyway, we brought lunch."

Nellie stared. "Burger King? We're in Austria, land of schnitzel, sauerbraten, white asparagus, and the greatest pastry in the world, and you bought American fast food? I'd expect it from Dan, but you, Amy?"

Dan took a burger, turned on the TV, and flopped on the couch. "White asparagus! Green wasn't gross enough. Soggy cigars, man."

The monitor brightened. The image crackled and sharpened. Three jaws dropped.

Larger than life at the center of the screen was an attractive teenager, resplendent in the latest hip-hop fashion. Smiling with all thirty-two gleaming white teeth, he was holding a press conference, and the gaggle of reporters and throng of adoring fans were lapping it up. The teen was completely comfortable with his fame, and why not? He had the top-rated reality TV show in the world, the number-one single on the pop charts, a bestselling clothing line, a series of popular children's books, action figures, souvenir steak knives, and even his own Pez dispenser.

His name was Jonah Wizard: international star and mogul, Cahill cousin, rival in the search for the 39 Clues.

"Jonah!" Amy exclaimed, her brow furrowed with worry. It unnerved her to think of their competition. The others seemed to have so much going for them—fame, brawn, experience, training, and lots and lots of money. How could a couple of no-name orphans expect to compete with that? She squinted at the date stamp in the bottom corner of the screen. "This was recorded yesterday! What's he doing in Vienna?"

"He's on a promotional tour," supplied Nellie. "The European DVD of *Who Wants to Be a Gangsta?* comes out this week."

"That's just a cover!" Dan exclaimed. "He's here because he knows the next clue is about Mozart. Maybe he found something we missed in Paris."

"Or he's working with the Holts," Nellie added. "They must have checked where our train was headed."

Amy peered at her famous cousin on TV. Why did that street seem so familiar? Suddenly, she understood. "Dan—it's Domgasse!"

Dan stared. "You're right! There's the Mozarthaus a couple of doors down! And look—it's that old librarian, the one who called out the SWAT team over a missing diary!"

Nellie frowned at the elderly Austrian woman on the stoop. "Not my idea of the classic hip-hop fan."

Amy shrugged. "I suppose anybody would be interested to check out such a big star —" Her breath caught in her throat. "Guys, I've got it! What if it's no accident Jonah picked that spot for his press conference? What if he did it there to create a distraction so he could steal Nannerl's diary from the Mozarthaus?"

"That would make sense," Dan mused, "except there he is on-screen, with twenty cameras on him, stealing nothing."

Amy shook her head. "When have we ever seen Jonah without his father standing right behind him, talking into two cell phones and making business deals on his BlackBerry? So where's Daddy at this press conference?"

Dan clued in. "Jonah held the conference to give his dad the chance to sneak into the Mozarthaus and swipe the diary! Amy, you were right — the diary *is* important!"

"Yeah, and now the enemy has it."

"That stinks," Dan agreed. "We were just a day late. Still . . ." His eyes took on a glitter of inspiration. "They stole it from the museum; why can't we steal it from them?"

"Hang on," Nellie burst in. "There's a big difference between searching for clues and robbing people. You're not crooks."

"But Jonah and his dad are," Dan argued. "If we're going to compete with them, we have to be willing to do what they do."

Nellie was unmoved. "As long as I'm your babysitter—"

"Au pair!" Dan interjected hotly.

"—I'm not going to stand by and let you two switch over to the dark side."

"But then we'll *lose*!" Dan wailed.

Amy spoke up, her expression solemn. "As much as I hate to agree with Dan, he's got a point. I know stealing is wrong, but this contest is too huge for us to worry about being the good guys. A chance to influence human history—we could change the whole world!"

"It *might* be a chance to change the world," Nellie amended. "That's what Mr. McIntyre said. He also said trust nobody—and that includes him."

Sudden tears filled Amy's eyes and she blinked them back stubbornly. This was too important to blur with her blubbering. "We barely knew our parents before they died. Grace was all we had, and now she's gone, too. The contest is a big deal for everybody, but for us, it's all we have. We can't do this halfway. We have to go all out. And that means looking for clues wherever they are—even inside somebody else's hotel room."

Nellie remained silent. Amy swallowed hard and went on. "You're not a Cahill, so you shouldn't have to put yourself at risk. But if you can't live with what we need to do, we'll just have to find a way to go on without you."

Dan goggled at his sister. The road that lay ahead would instantly become twenty times more difficult, complicated, and dangerous without their au pair. The cover of an adult was essential to every step they took, every border they crossed, every hotel room they rented. They were already the underdogs of this contest. Alone, they would need miracles just to move from place to place, and day to day.

Nellie regarded the Cahill kids. She was used to Dan's impulsiveness, but Amy was the most sensible fourteen-year-old she'd ever known. All at once, she was overcome by a surge of affection and pride.

"You think you can get rid of me that easily?" she demanded. "Fat chance. This may be your show, but I still make the rules. No way am I going to let you burgle a superstar without me. Pull up a chair—we've got a heist to plan."

The Royal Hapsburg Hotel was located at the heart of Vienna's Landstrasse district, the center of Austria's power elite. The building had once been a royal palace in the old Austro-Hungarian Empire, and floodlights made the white marble and gold leaf gleam against the night sky.

"How do we know this is his hotel?" Dan asked as they circled the block.

"Simple," Amy told him. "It's the snootiest, fanciest, most expensive place in town. Where else would he be?" She pointed to the hotel's magnificent entrance, where reporters and photographers swarmed. "Proof enough?"

"The launch party for Jonah's new DVD is at eight," Nellie put in. "He'll probably come down, talk with reporters for a few minutes, and then head over to Eurotainment TV, which is hosting the bash. In the paper, they said everybody who's anybody is going to be there."

Dan made a face. "I thought you quit being a Jonah Wizard fan when he dissed you in Paris."

"I'm helping you rob the guy, aren't I? What I'm saying is when he shows up down here, that means it's safe to get into his room."

As if on cue, a white chauffeur-driven Bentley whispered up to the curb and sat there, awaiting its Very Important Passenger. There was a stir in the crowd of media people, and the star himself emerged from his hotel, his ever-present father a half step behind him. Camera flashes lit up the night.

"Quick!" hissed Amy. "We can't let him see us!"

They ducked behind a magazine kiosk and watched Jonah work the crowd.

"Whassup, yo? . . . Thanks for coming out . . . 'Preciate that . . . Word."

Behind him, his father's thumbs were just a blur as he text messaged on his BlackBerry, probably sharing his son's eloquence with the world.

The media scrum began peppering the star with questions.

"Jonah, can we expect any surprises on the European version of the DVD?"

"Any truth to the rumor that you're dating Miley Cyrus?"

"Have you heard that the kung fu grip on your action figure flunked safety inspection?"

Jonah answered these in his usual style, somehow managing to sound urban hip and folksy at the same time.

Amy didn't like him, but she couldn't help marveling at his ease and skill dealing with the paparazzi. It went beyond merely coming up with the right things to say. Jonah made the press *love* him.

I'm the total opposite of that, she reflected. Just the thought of speaking to a large crowd terrified her.

"Hey, Jonah," a reporter called. "You're on top of the world at fifteen. Do you worry that you've got nowhere to go but down?"

The man of the hour grinned. "Chill out, yo. Who says I'm on top? I'm not even top banana in this hotel. Man, the Grand Duke of Luxembourg is staying right here. Don't get me wrong, I'm pretty happening. But doesn't royalty beat having your own Pez dispenser?"

"Let's go," muttered Nellie. "His modesty is turning my stomach."

As Jonah continued to charm the crowd, the Cahills and Nellie stole around the corner and slipped into the hotel through a side entrance.

They walked past a bank of ornate gold elevators and ducked through a door marked with a sign in German.

"*Employees only,*" Nellie translated in a whisper.

"You speak German?" Amy hissed in surprise.

"It's more like a working knowledge," she replied with a shrug. "Look—the freight elevator."

They rode down to the basement level, where they found a maze of corridors.

Amy was fearful of being approached from around every corner and behind every door. Her dread chilled her from within, as if her spine had been infused with liquid nitrogen. The cellar was cold, but not enough to explain her shivering.

"Why is it so empty?" she asked finally.

"Most of the staff works the day shift," Nellie guessed. "Jackpot!" she added, leading them through a partition into what looked like a dressing room. She selected a chambermaid's uniform from a large rack, ducked behind a divider, and quickly changed into it.

"Maybe we should lose the nose ring," Amy suggested timidly.

"Nothing doing," Nellie replied. "The stuffed shirts in this place need a little livening up. Come on." She jammed her regular clothes, then both Amy and Dan, into a housekeeping cart. An armload of sheets and towels went on top to conceal her passengers.

"How do we know what room he's in?" Dan whispered from the depths of the pile as Nellie rolled them back toward the elevator.

"The royal suite, of course," Nellie murmured. "Would anything less be good enough for that stuck-up nitwit? And keep it down. Laundry doesn't talk."

The elevator took them to the top floor, the seventeenth. Nellie pushed the cart down the hall, stopping in front of suite 1700, the one with the gilt crown prominently displayed over the door. Knowing that the Wizards were on their way to their party, she boldly plucked the key card out of its tray and inserted it into the reader.

A beep, a green light, and they were inside.

"Wow," the au pair breathed. "So this is Lifestyles of the Rich and Famous."

The room was palatial, with museum-quality furniture and decorative pieces — sofas and lounges in the nineteenth-century style, soft and overstuffed and upholstered in plush velvet; delicate china lamps and vases; everything oozing opulent taste.

She reached down and was in the process of pulling the Cahills out of their hiding place, when a heavily accented voice inquired, "Does a maid not knock at His Highness's door?"

CHAPTER 5

Shocked, Nellie pushed her charges back down among the linen. "Uh—I'm sorry," she managed. "I thought the suite was empty. I'm supposed to bring fresh towels to the Wizards' room."

"My dear young lady, this is the suite of his Highness the Grand Duke of Luxembourg." The man's lip curled slightly. "The American television actor is in the suite below—and a great fuss he made about that, I might add."

Nellie began backing the cart toward the door. "Sorry, sir. I'll get out of your way."

"A moment, if you please. Now that you are here, His Highness's bedchamber requires refreshing."

Nellie continued backing away. "Well, I really should get down to the Wizards' . . ."

"Nonsense. It will take but a moment. And there are several other matters that require your attention. If you'll follow me to the bathroom . . ."

"Coming," she called after him. She leaned down into the linen bin, thrust the key card into the nearest hand, and whispered, "When you hear my voice in the next room, *get out of here!*"

"What about you?" Amy squeaked.

"I can handle myself. You get the diary. I'll meet you back at our hotel. Be careful!"

And she was gone. A moment later, they could hear her announcing loudly, "This bathroom is bigger than my whole apartment!"

The sheets began flying, and Amy and Dan scrambled from the cart and slipped through the door into the hallway.

"Jonah's one floor down," Dan rasped.

They ran for the stairs.

The door of suite 1600 was identical to its upstairs counterpart, except there was no crown.

"Poor Jonah," Amy said sarcastically as they let themselves in with the key card. "He's really slumming it."

If the rooms were any less opulent than the Grand Duke's accomodations, Amy and Dan couldn't tell where corners had been cut. The suite was massive and elegantly decorated. The marble floor gleamed; the rich carpets were hand-woven and luxurious. Every vase and ashtray on every end table looked like it had been placed there by an artist.

"Kind of makes our place in Boston seem like an outhouse," Dan observed.

Amy sighed. "I don't care about the high life. But sometimes it bugs me just how *rich* the competition is."

"Grace was rich." Dan's brow clouded as he remembered the fire that had destroyed their grandmother's mansion on the day of her funeral. "Anyway, I'd rather be poor and normal than a rich idiot like Jonah or the Cobras."

"Yeah, but money is a big advantage in a contest like this," his sister argued bleakly. "It can open a lot of doors that we'll have to find another way around. We're really outclassed, Dan."

"That's what cheating is for." He surveyed the expansive parlor. "Now, if I was a stuck-up idiot with my head on a Pez dispenser, where would I hide the diary I jacked?"

Amy smiled in spite of herself. "We'd better search the whole place."

They began to comb the huge suite, looking under sofa cushions, in drawers, behind drapes, and through closets.

"Hey, check it out." Dan reached into a small carton and withdrew a six-inch-tall action figure, Jonah Wizard in plasticized Phat Farm jeans and warm-up jacket. "Not a very good likeness," he commented. "He's much uglier in real life."

"Put that back!" hissed Amy, rifling through a drawer. "It's bad enough we broke into his room. We don't need to steal his dumb toys."

"It's for my collection," Dan protested. "He's got a whole box of them. Hey—this must be the one with the kung fu grip." He pressed the button and watched the tiny fist snap closed. "Whoa—no wonder it's being recalled! You could crack a walnut with this thing!"

"Look!" Amy's eyes danced with excitement. She turned the toy around in Dan's hand. When the grip was activated, a sequence of red letters and numbers lit up on the back of the figure's headband. "GR63K1!" she read breathlessly. "It's some kind of secret code!"

Dan snorted a laugh in her face. "For a straight-A student, you can be pretty dumb. Sure, it's a code—to download a free Jonah Wizard screen saver from his website! The commercials are all over TV back home."

His sister reddened. "I guess I'm not as much of a couch potato as you," she mumbled in embarrassment, and returned her attention to the search. Dan stuffed the figure in his pocket and joined her.

The suite had five rooms—the parlor, two bedrooms, a dressing chamber, and the kitchen. They went through every inch of the place, with no results. The master bedroom had a safe, but it was unlocked and empty. Even an examination of the kitchen and minibar revealed nothing.

"You don't think he's got it with him, do you?" Dan asked in alarm.

His sister shook her head. "You don't bring a hot item like that to a place where every TV camera in Europe is pointed at you. It's here. We just have to find it."

"Where do we look?" Dan was running out of patience. "It's too dark, anyway! What's up with these fancy hotels putting twenty layers of drapes over all the windows?" He flipped a light switch. A vast crystal chandelier blazed overhead.

Amy and Dan gasped. At the center of this confection of light hung a basket formed by ropes of crystals. There, dark against the brilliance, was the unmistakable silhouette of a book.

"The diary!" they chorused.

Dan ran for a chair.

"Not high enough!" his sister barked. "Come help me with the table."

They took the heavy glass table and hauled it under the chandelier. Dan climbed atop it, but he was still too short. "Hand me the chair."

Soon, Amy was perched on the table, steadying the chair and her brother, who stood on tiptoe atop two phone books on the seat.

Straining to reach through the strings of crystals, Dan felt his hand close on the leather-bound cover. "Got it!"

He drew out the diary of Maria Anna "Nannerl" Mozart.

The job of au pair to the Cahill kids had brought Nellie experiences that she never could have anticipated. This was one of them—crawling on her hands and knees in a marble bathroom, scrubbing a grand duke's toilet.

No way there's mildew in here, she thought bitterly. But maybe royalty could detect stains regular people couldn't see, kind of like "The Princess and the Pea."

"The Grand Duke and the Bowl." Catchy title.

One thing was certain. Amy and Dan owed her big for this. She wondered if they had managed to find the diary yet. If only there were some way of knowing that the mission had been accomplished. Then she could conk the Grand Duke's assistant with the toilet brush and get out of this five-star freak show.

Her brow clouded as the vision grew darker—Amy and Dan, caught, arrested, or worse. Who knew what dangers were lurking out there in this winner-take-all game? Hotel security was scary enough, but those crazy Cahill cousins were capable of anything! The winner of this contest might literally rule the world. A lot of nut jobs had done some terrible things with that kind of power as a prize. What chance did two young kids have?

Her uneasy thoughts popped like a soap bubble when an unfriendly voice over her shoulder announced, "You do not work for us, *Fräulein*. What are you doing in this suite?"

Heart sinking, Nellie turned around. Next to the Grand Duke's man was a uniformed guard.

She tried to bluff it through. "Of course I work here. Do you think I sneak into hotels for the pleasure of scrubbing strangers' toilets?"

"You do not work here," the man repeated humorlessly.

"You know every single employee?" she challenged.

"No," he admitted. "You have the earring in the nose. It is against hotel policy. You will come with me."

Nellie thought hard. She wasn't sure how much trouble she was in. She was a foreigner in this country. If she ended up deported, what would happen to Amy and Dan?

"All right, you caught me. I'm here by mistake. I was trying to get into Jonah Wizard's suite. I'm his biggest fan. I just *have* to meet him! But I picked the wrong room."

The man's eyes probed hers. "And you are doing this crime alone? No one is with you?"

"I'm totally alone," she said, perhaps too quickly. "And it's not a crime to love Jonah Wizard. He's just the coolest—"

From directly below, an enormous crash shook the building.

The security man looked daggers at Nellie. "The Wizard suite! *Fräulein*, you had better hope that this disturbance has nothing to do with you, or you will be enjoying a great deal more of our Austrian hospitality."

"Dan, are you all right?"

Dan lay on the floor of the suite, in the wreckage of the chair, in the wreckage of the table.

He groaned and sat up, the diary clutched in his arms like a football. "What happened?"

"I'm not sure," Amy replied, none too steady herself. She hauled him to his feet and scanned him for cuts. "Either the chair broke and dropped us through the table, or the table broke first, and that's what broke the chair. It doesn't matter. We've got to get out of here—half the hotel must have heard that crash!"

They ran out of suite 1600 just as a uniformed security officer burst from the stairwell, pulling none other than Nellie with him.

There was no chance of feigning cluelessness. The door was still open behind them, the wreckage clearly visible from the hall.

The Cahills fled, sprinting around the nearest corner and out of view. The guard moved to give chase, but Nellie grabbed his arm and pulled him back with a heave that almost dislocated his shoulder.

"You can't leave! What if Jonah is lying in there, bleeding?"

The security man was in a towering rage. "Stupid girl! Your hero is not even in the building!" He took a walkie-talkie from his belt and began speaking in rapid-fire German.

Nellie swallowed the lump in her throat. He was placing a guard at the elevators and at the bottom of all building stairwells.

Amy and Dan were trapped.

CHAPTER 6

When the elevator door rolled open, both Cahills were running so hard that they almost blasted straight past it. Amy put the brakes on first, grabbed her brother, and hauled him aboard. She pressed L. They stood, chests heaving, as the car descended. Their anxious eyes followed the readout as the numbers counted down from sixteen.

Suddenly, Dan's hand snaked out and pressed 2. "They could be waiting for us in the lobby," he explained tensely.

"But that's where the exit is!" Amy shrilled. "You can't leave from the second floor!"

"Sure you can." The doors opened, and Dan pulled her out onto 2, amid ballrooms and meeting facilities.

She was nearly hysterical. "How?"

"By jumping."

Amy stared at him. "Have you lost your—"

They snaked around a bend in the corridor, and the hotel's front drive appeared before them through floor-to-ceiling glass.

Dan pushed open the French doors, and the two stepped out onto a narrow stone balcony.

"No way, Dan! I'm not jumping! We'll break our legs!"

"Look down!" he commanded.

Six feet below stretched a canvas awning that ran across the front entrance.

He swung a leg over the stone railing. "Piece of cake," he said, trying to sound more certain than he felt. "A shorter drop than the high diving board."

"But no water!"

He dropped. Amy watched in horror, expecting him to tear through the fabric and be dashed to pieces on the concrete. Instead, the awning held.

Grinning up at her, he crawled to the edge of the canvas, found a steel support, and shinnied to the sidewalk. He waved at her with Nannerl's diary.

Never had Amy experienced fear on so many different levels all at the same time — fear of capture; fear for Nellie; fear for her crazy brother, who was too stupid to know what couldn't be done; and a very real fear of stepping off a second-story balcony onto a fragile piece of cloth.

"Hurry up!" came an impatient call from below.

I can't do it . . . I just can't . . .

The flood of shame was almost as overwhelming as her terror. Some Cahill she turned out to be! The future of the entire world was at stake, and she couldn't cajole herself into a six-foot drop — not even after seeing her eleven-year-old brother do it. She might as well let Jonah have the diary. Or the Holts or the Kabras. Her grandmother had been wrong about her. She didn't have what it took.

Sorry, Grace . . .

It was this thought that jolted Amy into sudden explosive action. She was already falling through the air before she'd actually come to the decision to do it. She hit the fabric like an errant trapeze artist into a safety net. Seconds later, Dan was hauling her down to the street.

They were in a taxi and blocks away before either of them dared to speak.

"Nellie—" Dan began.

"I know . . ."

Their little room at the Hotel Franz Josef seemed dingy and even smaller after the accommodations at the Royal Hapsburg. The greeting they received from Saladin didn't help their general mood. The Egyptian Mau still refused cat food, and, in fact, had spread his dinner all over the carpet. A fishy smell hung in the air. In addition, the scratching had gotten worse than ever and was beginning to wear away the fur around his collar.

Both Cahills were exhausted, but neither thought of sleep. Nellie was all that was important now. They'd been so focused on the 39 Clues that they hadn't considered how much their au pair was giving up to stick with them and their quest. She had put her life on hold, traveled thousands of miles from home, and even charged many of their expenses on her personal credit card. Sure, they planned to pay her back. Amy and Dan had jewelry from Grace that was probably worth a lot of money. But jewelry could be lost or stolen, and there was no guarantee that they would win the contest. There was no guarantee that they would even survive it.

Now Nellie was missing — caught, probably under arrest. And there was nothing Amy and Dan could do about it. Nothing but wait.

At two A.M., they were still sitting, staring at the TV, which featured a *Gilligan's Island* episode dubbed in German. The sudden knocking was such a jolt to their frayed nerves that they almost tackled each other running to answer the door.

"Nellie!" Amy cried. "Thank—"

There in the hall stood Irina Spasky, a Russian Cahill cousin. Another competitor in the search for the 39 Clues, and no joke. Irina was rumored to be an ex-KGB agent, ruthless, efficient, and potentially deadly.

She got right to the point. "Your nanny has been detained by Viennese authorities."

Dan bristled. "How do you know that?"

Irina's face contorted into the closest she ever came to a smile. "I have accompanied weapons-grade plutonium through a secret tunnel under the Berlin Wall. I believe I am capable of looking through the window of a police car. But if you do not need my help—"

Amy seized on this. "You can help Nellie? How?"

Irina looked annoyed. "What is it your business, so long as she is returned to you?"

"It's not our business at all!" Amy agreed swiftly. "Just get her out! Thank you!"

"I require better thanks than just words. Shall we say the item you removed from the hotel room of our obnoxious cousin Jonah Wizard?"

"No deal!" Dan barked.

"A word of advice," Irina told Amy. "You should not let this impetuous little boy speak for you. Perhaps you should not let him speak at all. In the KGB, we found duct tape to be both effective and affordable."

Amy hung her head. They had risked their lives to get the diary. Not to mention the fact that Irina wanting it only proved their suspicion that it was important. But they couldn't let Nellie go to jail for them. If their Russian cousin could free her, they had no choice but to make the deal.

"I'll get it for you," Amy agreed sadly.

"*I'll* get it," sighed Dan.

Amy watched in surprise as her brother went to her backpack on the nightstand. But instead of taking out the Nannerl diary, he reached into his jacket pocket and produced the Jonah Wizard action figure he had taken from suite 1600.

He's trying to give her the wrong thing! Amy struggled to contain her terror as Dan offered the toy to Irina.

The ex-KGB agent made no move to accept it. "A child's plaything? You are not serious."

Dan shrugged. "You asked for what we took out of Jonah's room. This is it."

Don't try it! Amy wanted to scream. *What if Irina knows what she's looking for?* She stared imploringly at her brother.

He didn't pick up on the message. "It only *seems* like an action figure," he told Irina. "Check *this* out." He held the toy so that the tiny hand wrapped around her little finger and pressed the button on Jonah's back to activate the kung fu grip.

The former spy did not utter a sound, but a vein on her forehead stood out and bulged as if it were about to explode. Her eyes fell eagerly upon the website code illuminated at the back of Jonah's headband.

"See?" asked Dan. "It's —"

"There is no need for small talk in a business transaction." She snatched the figure from Dan and regarded it with newfound respect. "We had a similar device in the KGB," she admitted, examining her rapidly swelling pinkie. "Crude but effective. Expect your nanny shortly." And she was gone as quickly as she had appeared.

Amy was shaking as she wheeled on her brother. "I can't believe you did that! What if Irina knew about the diary?"

"She didn't," Dan retorted.

"But she could have! Or the code! She might have seen the commercial about the screen saver!"

He was serene. "I doubt Irina watches much Cartoon Network."

"You ripped off a Russian spy! You could have gotten Nellie killed, and maybe us, too!"

Dan was outraged. "Why are you yelling at me about what didn't happen? In case you haven't noticed, I did something *good*! We've still got the diary, and Irina is going to spring Nellie. Do you think it'll be a real prison break? Too bad we can't watch."

Amy looked grim. "I honestly don't want to think about what a KGB agent is capable of. Whatever she can do to the Viennese police she can turn on *us* at any moment."

He couldn't hold back a grin. "But right now, tonight, we got the better of her. That's something to celebrate!"

"Who's celebrating?" came a weary voice from the doorway.

"Nellie!" Amy bounded over and threw her arms around the au pair. She took a step back, frowning. "How did Irina get you out so fast? She just left five minutes ago."

"Nobody got me out," Nellie replied. "They just let me go. They think I'm a deranged Jonah Wizard fan. Apparently, the hotel's full of them. A couple of idiots actually jumped off the front balcony. Can you picture that?"

"In Technicolor," Amy said bitterly.

"That low-down KGB reject!" Dan fumed. "I can't believe she cheated me — right when I was in the middle of cheating her!"

"Anyway, it's been a long night." Nellie yawned. "Those get-a-lifers at the hotel wouldn't part with their precious maid's uniform, so the cops had to drag me over there to hunt down my clothes from that cart — which was back in the basement with fifty others. Then I didn't want to lead them to you, so I had them drop me off at the Hotel Wiener. I've been walking ever since. But don't worry — it only rained for the last half mile." She toweled her hair off with her sleeve. "Is it just me, or does it smell like fish in here?"

"We got the diary," Amy told her excitedly. "Let's get some sleep, and we can look at it tomorrow morning. We know the Holts, Irina, and Jonah are just a heartbeat away from us. We've got to move fast if we're going to stay ahead."

When Jonah Wizard and his father returned flushed with victory from the DVD launch party, they found a team of maintenance people sweeping glass fragments from the marble floor of their suite.

Both ran to stand directly beneath the chandelier where they had hidden Nannerl's diary. The dark shape was no longer there. A few strands of crystals hung broken.

"You promised Jonah extra security!" Mr. Wizard raged at the hotel manager, who had gotten out of bed to apologize to this very important guest.

"We believe it was harmless, *mein Herr*," the manager soothed. "A lovesick girl. Your talented son has this effect on the young ladies, yes?"

The Wizards didn't believe a word of it. It was no mere fan who had broken into the suite and stolen Nannerl Mozart's diary. This could only be the work of one of their 39 Clues competitors. A Cahill inside job.

"Yo, man." The TV star addressed the hotel manager directly. "How about you describe this stalker chick who loves me so much she broke into my crib."

The manager held up a mug shot from the Vienna police department.

The famous face creased into a frown. When you kicked back with Hollywood A-listers and the giga-celebrity crowd, it was tough to recognize your average nobody off the street. Yet the woman in the picture looked sort of familiar. Why did Jonah know that person?

Then he noticed the nose ring. It was the Cahill kids' nursemaid—Nancy or Netta, something like that.

So Amy and Dan had made it to Vienna, too. Worse, they'd turned out to be a step ahead of him. Jonah Wizard didn't like to be second best at anything. Not in the TV ratings, not on the pop charts, and definitely not in the contest.

When you're on top, you've got the confidence. The confidence gives you the attitude. And the attitude is what keeps you on top.

A twinge of misgiving vibrated in the deepest, darkest recess of his mind. Yeah, he was number one across the board, dominating just about every category of the entertainment industry. And he *deserved* that success. He'd *earned* it. Sweat and hard work, man. Talent. That Wizard mojo.

But it doesn't hurt when your mom is Cora Wizard, with mucho connections in every field of the arts. . . .

The megastar grimaced. *This* was why he could never let his guard down! One little setback, and he was already starting to doubt himself.

If you lose—even once—it becomes a habit. And before you know it, you're a loser.

He couldn't allow the Cahill kids to get the better of him.

Luckily, he knew something about the diary that Amy and Dan still had to find out.

CHAPTER 7

Diaries were not Dan's thing — not even when they were in English and written by people he cared about. He kept his distance, trying to interest Saladin in a tin of tuna fish, while Nellie and Amy huddled over the leather-bound journal. Nellie was translating Maria Anna Mozart's flowery, old-fashioned script.

"Anything good?" he called to them.

"It's a tragedy," Amy replied. "Nannerl was one of the greatest musicians of her time. And yet very few people have even heard of her. She was a great genius — every bit as brilliant as her brother. But in those days, girls were just supposed to get married, and cook, and clean, and have babies."

Dan looked disinterested. "I never heard of her brother, either — not until this contest. I mean, I've heard of *Baby Mozart* — you know, the video —"

Nellie scowled in his direction. "You'd still recognize a lot of his music. We're talking about some of the most famous melodies of all time. Even 'Twinkle, Twinkle, Little Star' — the music to that was written by Mozart."

"You can only guess what Nannerl might have contributed if she'd been allowed to develop her talents," Amy added.

"I don't care about music," countered Dan. "Did she contribute clues?"

Amy shook her head. "There are no notes scribbled in the margins or anything like that."

"There's a letter from her brother pasted in here," Nellie supplied, "but it seems like he's talking about the time he quit his job. He said he wanted to use his contract as toilet paper."

"Really?" Dan was suddenly interested. "Mozart said that? Show me!"

"It's in German, dweeb," his sister told him. "They have a word for toilet paper, too."

"Yeah, but I didn't think a fancy guy like Mozart would know it."

"Hold it!" Amy's voice was full of alarm. She turned the next leaf, peering intently at the spine of the notebook. "There are pages missing here! At least two. Look!"

The three examined the diary closely. Amy was right. The thief had been extra careful to disguise his crime — the missing material had been cut out with a very sharp blade. The excision was almost unnoticeable.

"Do you think Jonah did it?" Dan breathed.

"I doubt it," Amy replied. "Why would he bother to hide the diary in the chandelier if he'd already taken the important parts out of it?"

"To throw us off the trail of the real stuff?" Dan suggested.

"Maybe, but remember — this book is over two hundred years old. Those pages could have been removed any time between then and now. For all we know, Nannerl cut them out herself because she spilled ink on them."

"No offense, you guys," Nellie put in, "but I've been around your family long enough to know this has Cahill written all over it. I've never seen such a bunch of backstabbers in my life."

"She's right," Dan said glumly. "Every time we think we're making progress on the thirty-nine clues, someone turns out to be a step ahead of us."

"Calm down," Amy told him. "The real clue isn't the diary; it's the music. And we're the only ones who have that. Let's take it down to the lobby. I saw a piano there."

They made a charming picture — the American girl at the piano and her younger brother at her side. It would have been nit-picking to notice that the sheet music was written on the back of a Eurail napkin, and that the girl played falteringly.

"Good old Aunt Beatrice," Amy murmured to Dan. "She cut off my piano lessons so she could pinch a few more pennies."

Aunt Beatrice was their grandmother's sister and their legal guardian. It was thanks to Aunt

Beatrice that Amy and Dan were now fugitives from Social Services in the Commonwealth of Massachusetts.

"Play the new stuff," Dan suggested. "The part that isn't in the real song. Maybe a trapdoor will open, or we'll call up the Cahill genie or something."

She tried it, a light, airy melody, very different from the heavier classical piece around it. Suddenly, there was a woman standing beside the piano, lifting her voice in song. The lyrics were German, but it was obvious that the tune was familiar and brought the lady pleasure.

"You know this song!" Amy exclaimed. "Is it by Mozart?"

"*Nein* — not Mozart. It is an old Austrian folk song called '*Der Ort, wo ich geboren war.*' This means in your language 'The Place Where I Was Born.' Thank you for playing it, my dear. I haven't heard it for many years."

Amy grabbed Dan and hauled him to the privacy of a small alcove with a fireplace. "That's it! That's the clue!"

"What? Some old song?"

"It was a message between Mozart and Ben Franklin!"

Dan was bug-eyed. "Okay, but what does it say?"

"It says 'come to the place where I was born.' Mozart was born in the town of Salzburg, in the Austrian Alps. And that's where we have to go."

The rental car was an old Fiat that squeaked in every joint and didn't like going up Alps but didn't mind coasting down the other side of them. Part of this might have been Nellie's fault. She'd never driven a stick shift before.

"That's just great for a trip into the mountains," Dan complained.

"Hey—you want to get behind the wheel?" Nellie demanded, insulted. And Dan said yes so readily that she was sorry she'd asked.

Saladin spent the entire three-hour drive carsick. But luckily, since the cat wasn't eating anything, he also had nothing to throw up.

The trip would have been roomier and much more pleasant on the train. But their encounter with the Holts on the ride from Paris had soured them on travel by rail. On a public train, they were too easy to spot. They could be more anonymous in a car. With the latest lead in their hands and theirs only, surely all the other teams would be gunning for them.

Despite the uneven ride, the scenery was spectacular. The autobahn wound through the Austrian Alps like a ribbon twisting among the feet of giants. Soon their necks ached from craning out the windows, gazing up at dizzying snowcapped peaks.

"Now *this* is more like it," Nellie approved. "I came on this trip to see the world, not the inside of a Vienna police station."

Even Dan was impressed by the soaring mountains. "I'll bet if you roll a snowball off the top, by the time it gets to the bottom, it could knock out a whole town!"

Shortly after two, they reached Salzburg — a small city of gleaming spires, baroque architecture, and picturesque gardens nestled in green hills.

"It's beautiful!" breathed Nellie.

"It's bigger than I expected," Amy put in ruefully. "We have no idea what we're looking for, or even where to start."

Nellie shrugged. "Seems pretty straightforward. The song is 'The Place Where I Was Born.' We'll get a guidebook and find the actual house where Mozart grew up."

The moaning from Dan was even louder and more pitiful than Saladin's constant complaining. "Oh, no you don't. You're not dragging me to another Mozart house. Not when I haven't even recovered from the last one!"

"Grow up," Amy said sharply. "We're not tourists. We go where the clues are."

"How come the clues are never in the local laser tag place?" Dan whined. He sat up suddenly. *"Look out!"*

A pedestrian rushed into the road right in front of the Fiat. Nellie stomped on the brake with all her might.

The wheels locked, and the car skidded to a halt mere inches from mowing down the elderly jaywalker.

Nellie was almost berserk. "Moron!" She brought her arm forward to deliver a blast on the horn.

Amy grabbed her wrist. "Don't!" she hissed, trying to duck behind the dash. "Look who that is!"

CHAPTER 8

Three pairs of eyes focused on the tall, straight-backed Asian man hurrying across the street, tapping along with his diamond-tipped walking stick.

Alistair Oh, their Korean cousin, yet another competitor in the contest.

"So much for us being ahead of the other teams," Dan observed.

"He's probably not here for the clear mountain air," Nellie agreed.

They watched as Uncle Alistair loped across the street and boarded a bus parked at the opposite curb.

"Follow him," Amy said suddenly. "Let's see where he's going."

Nellie made a highly illegal right turn from the left lane and fell into line behind the bus. She waved gaily at the Salzburg drivers who were cursing and honking.

"You know," mused Dan, "if we want to find out where he's going, why can't we just ask the guy? Don't we still have an alliance with him from Paris?"

"Remember what Mr. McIntyre said," Amy countered. "Trust no one."

"Maybe so. But Uncle Alistair sure saved our butts in the Catacombs."

Amy was unimpressed. "Only because he had to help us to stop the Kabras. If there's one thing we ought to know by now, it's that Cahills have been fighting each other for centuries. He'd do anything to distract us from the thirty-nine clues."

They followed the bus as it rattled over the Staatsbrucke — the bridge at the center of town. Passengers got on, but no one got off. The streets were crowded with cars and taxis, and throngs of sightseers were everywhere. A high school group stepped out in front of the Fiat, and the bus roared around a corner and out of view.

"Don't lose them," Dan said urgently.

At last, the road cleared, and the Fiat lurched off, Nellie shifting awkwardly. They jounced down a few narrow streets, but there was no sign of the bus.

Amy pointed. "There!"

The bus had left the grid of downtown streets and was roaring around the side of a hill. In a screech of gears, they set off in pursuit, picking up speed as the Fiat rounded the bend. They were so focused on the chase that they raced right past the stopped bus, which was disgorging passengers at an ancient stone gate.

Amy peered at the collection of very old buildings topped with steeples and crosses. "A church?"

Dan looked miserable. "Like Mozart wasn't boring enough."

"The last church we were in wasn't boring," Amy reminded him. "We both nearly got killed."

Nellie made a U-turn and pulled up a discreet distance behind the bus. "St. Peter's Archabbey," she translated, squinting at the wrought-iron sign.

They could see Alistair's tall figure starting up the sloped path through the gate.

Nellie frowned. "Do you think your clue could be in there?"

"Alistair thinks it is," Amy decided. "We can't leave until we know one way or the other. Why don't you find a hotel and give Saladin a chance to recover from the trip?"

The au pair looked reluctant. Dan spoke up. "The place is full of tourists. How dangerous can it be?"

"All right," Nellie said finally. "I'll be back here in an hour. Try not to get yourselves killed." She drove off.

They entered through the gate, and Amy chose an English brochure from the rack. "Wow," she breathed. "This place is more than thirteen hundred years old. The monastery was founded in 696, but they think the Romans were here even before that."

"Romans?" Dan showed a stirring of interest. "Those Roman legions had some super-sweet fighting skills."

"That's why you find Roman artifacts all over Europe," Amy explained. "Their armies were so powerful that they conquered most of the known world."

"Unstoppable," Dan agreed. He frowned. "So why the church?"

"That was built later, in the twelfth century—long after the Romans had gone. The oldest graves in the cemetery date back to around that time."

"Cemetery?" Dan beamed. "This place is starting to grow on me!"

They lay low until Uncle Alistair's tour group had filed into the main cathedral and then ducked through the arch that led to the graveyard. It was like no cemetery Dan had ever seen—overgrown with brush, the markers barely visible through the foliage. Instead of tombstones, the plots were represented by wrought-iron signposts with fancy old-fashioned script.

"Reminds me of Aunt Beatrice's souvenir spoon collection," Dan mumbled to Amy.

Her nose was still immersed in the brochure. All at once, she grabbed his wrist and squeezed hard enough to splinter bone. "Dan—it says the last remains of Nannerl Mozart are right here!"

Dan's eyes widened. "We're going to dig up a dead body? *Awesome!*"

"Shhh! Of course not!"

"But what if Mozart planted a clue on his sister?"

Amy shook her head. "Mozart died *before* Nannerl. Now, we're looking for a communal tomb. That's where the guidebook says she's buried."

"What's that?" Dan asked. "Like a condo for dead people?"

"Show some respect. One of the others in her crypt is Michael Haydn, the famous composer, and one of Mozart's biggest supporters."

He couldn't resist. "What's he doing now — *de*composing?"

"Don't be gross. Come on."

It took a few minutes of wandering for them to find the mausoleum. Compared to some of the opulent and elaborate burial chambers at St. Peter's, it was a simple stone structure bearing the names of the dead with biblical passages engraved on the walls. There was no sign of anything that could be considered a clue.

"You're not forgotten, Nannerl," Amy whispered somberly. "People are starting to appreciate you as a genius in your own right."

"What's the big fascination with Nannerl Mozart?" Dan asked. "So she was as good as her brother. So what?"

"Don't you see how unfair that is?" Amy demanded. "She never got the credit just because she was a girl."

"I agree," said Dan. "She got a raw deal. But now that she's been in this crypt for a couple hundred years, what difference does it make to her?"

"It makes a difference to *me*," she argued. "What if we were the Mozart siblings? How do you think I'd feel if you were considered this whiz kid prodigy and I was nobody when we were equally good at the same thing?"

Her brother was unperturbed. "That could never happen to us. We're not good at *any* of the same things. Hey, what's that?"

He was peering quizzically out the crypt entrance. The abbey abutted a sheer rock face. Fifty feet off the ground, the rough outline of a building had been carved into the mountain. "Who puts a house halfway up a cliff?"

On closer inspection, they found a crude staircase hewn directly into the stone, leading to the cavelike portal.

Amy scoured the brochure. "Here it is. That's the entrance to the Salzburg Catacombs."

"Catacombs?" Dan echoed in trepidation. They had come very close to being lost forever in the Catacombs of Paris. He wasn't anxious for a repeat performance.

"Well, not the paved-with-bones kind," Amy explained. "But it says there are tunnels in that hill. If there's a clue at St. Peter's, I'll bet that's where it is."

A tour group came into view, working its way to the entrance on the cliff. In the middle of the cluster was the tall figure of Alistair Oh.

"And the competition just pulled ahead of us," Dan added.

As soon as Uncle Alistair's tour disappeared inside the rock face, the Cahills rushed up the uneven stone stairs. Amy felt a creepy unease as she stepped inside the mountain—as if they were being swallowed by something ancient and immutable, an immense, silent creature as old as the earth itself. Amy and Dan exchanged a look of pure dread. The Paris Catacombs had been lined with human bones, grotesque skulls leering from all directions. This may have been lower on the *ick* scale. But the sense of leaving the familiar for the freakish and threatening was even greater here.

The tunnel was clammy and easily twenty degrees colder than the outside.

Dan reached down and felt the familiar shape of his inhaler. This had to be the worst spot on earth for his asthma to flare up.

Chill out, he reminded himself. Attacks were brought on by extreme dust and pollen, not extreme creepiness.

To their left was a small cave chapel straight out of *The Flintstones.* Uncle Alistair's group was crowded in there when the Cahills hurried by, covering their faces.

The further they got from the entrance, the darker it became. The passage was lit only by a series of weak electric bulbs strung so far apart that everything faded to utter blackness in between them.

As they forged ahead, another tour group was walking toward them in the tunnel. Pale, top-lit faces vanished into the gloom only to reappear suddenly thirty feet closer. It was otherworldly — as if the laws of nature no longer applied in this alien place.

"Stay to the right," the tour guide ordered, directing his sightseers around the Cahills in the close quarters.

They were jostled by elbows and shoulders as the group shuffled past. Someone stepped on Amy's toe, and she drew in a sharp breath—or maybe her gasp was a reaction to the man she saw in the halo of the naked bulb.

He was old, older than Uncle Alistair, probably in his late sixties, with weathered, cratered skin. His clothing was all black, so his head appeared to be suspended in midair.

Amy's heart was thumping so hard that she was afraid it might punch clear through her ribcage. She grasped her brother's hand and began towing him along the passage.

"Slow down!" Dan complained.

Amy didn't stop until she was positive the tour group was out of earshot. "Dan—the m—the m—" Even whispering, she could not control her stammer.

"Calm down," her brother soothed.

"The man in black is here!"

CHAPTER 9

Dan was shocked. "Did he see you?"

"I'm not sure, but we can't take the chance. When Grace's house burned down, there he was. And when the bomb went off at the Franklin Institute. We've got to get out of here!"

"Not until we find what we came for," Dan said stubbornly. "Uncle Alistair *and* the man in black? That's *double* proof we're on the right track!"

Amy was surprised by the surge of admiration she felt. Sure, her brother was a dweeb who wouldn't last five minutes without her. But there were times — like now — that he found courage where she saw only fear.

She swallowed hard. "Let's keep going."

They forged deeper into the mountainside. The tunnel split and split again, and they made careful note of the twists and turns. Neither could think of anything more terrifying than getting lost back here, halfway between Salzburg and the earth's core.

The sting of eyestrain soon set in from scanning the endless walls for markings or coded symbols —

anything that might indicate a secret compartment or hiding place. Only rock greeted them, and the occasional trickle of water.

Dan was on his hands and knees, investigating a "carving" that turned out to be a groove in the stone, when the string of electric lights flickered once and went out.

Dark didn't even come close to describing it. They were plunged into suffocating blackness, a total absence of light. It was as if they had suddenly been struck blind.

The panic was like nothing Amy had experienced before. Her breath came out in gasps, faster and faster, as if the air she drew in was instantly sucked out of her.

Dan flailed his arms, reaching to reassure her. But when he touched her arm, she let out a shriek that echoed through the passageway in all directions.

"Calm down, it's me!" he hissed, although calm was the opposite of what he felt. "It's probably just a power failure!"

"And the man in black just *happens* to be here?" Amy squealed.

Dan struggled to think rationally. "If we can't see him, he can't see us, right? Who knows? Maybe he's just as lost as we are."

"And maybe he's back there somewhere, waiting for us."

He took a deep breath. "We'll have to chance it. All we can do is retrace our steps and hope for the best."

"Can we even find our way out?" she quavered.

Dan tried to visualize the tunnels as they might appear on a map — as intersecting lines. "You run your hand along one wall of the passage. I'll run my hand along the other. We won't miss any turns that way." He gulped. "Simple."

Simple. Oh, how Amy yearned for her brother's ability to reduce everything to a formula — a series of instructions to be followed. For her, no formula could ever be separated from the sheer terror of this darkness. She had a flashback to the Paris Catacombs, stacks of skulls grinning grotesquely at her. Yet at the same time she knew this was worse — the shaft much narrower, the walls pressing in on her, trapping her in the rock belly of this mountain.

"Dan, I don't think I can do this," she whimpered. "I'm just too scared."

"It's the same tunnel," he soothed. "We made it here; we can make it back."

They set out through the blackness. Amy felt her way along the left wall, knowing that Dan was doing the same on the right. They locked fingers to avoid losing each other and talked constantly to keep out the terror that would surely overwhelm them if it found a way in.

"Hey, Amy," said Dan, "when's the last time we held hands like this?"

"I can't remember. It had to be when we were little, little kids. You know — with Mom and Dad."

"What did Mom look like again?" He already knew the answer. He'd heard it at least a hundred times, yet the familiar conversation was comforting.

"She was tall," Amy replied, "with reddish-brown hair—"

"Like yours?" His standard question.

"Mom's was a bit redder. You couldn't miss her in the audience at a school play. Dad was fairer, with—" A pause. "It gets harder and harder to picture them both. Like an old snapshot where the image is fading."

"It stinks," muttered Dan. "Can't remember my own parents, but rotten Aunt Beatrice—she's a glowing electric billboard in my head."

"We've got Grace," Amy reminded him gently.

"Grace." The name came out as a sigh. "I miss her, but sometimes I wonder if I even should."

"Grace *loved* us."

"Then how come she didn't tell us about all this?" he demanded. "The Cahills! The contest! A little warning might've come in handy. Like, 'Okay, today you're a kid playing *Super Mario*, but in a couple of months you'll be lost in a European tunnel with a mad killer—'"

Bang!

The flash was a supernova in the blackness. Their eyes, wide-open, straining for night sight, were painfully overloaded. Dan could make out a figure running away from them in the passage. But his hands automatically snapped up to shield his face before he could make an ID. And then the explosion was over, replaced by the rumbling sound that signaled the ceiling was about to collapse.

Amy heard her brother's cry when the boulder struck his shoulder. Their hands were still clenched, so she felt it when he went down, buried by rocks and dirt.

"Dan!" She pulled his arm with all her might, even as she was pelted with falling gravel. Mustering a hidden cache of strength, she gave a mammoth yank, and her brother scrambled up beside her, spitting dust, unable to form words.

"Are you hurt?" she rasped.

Without answering, he reached into the blackness and felt along the outline of the rubble. It blocked the shaft completely. He tried to burrow through the pile, only to trigger a miniavalanche that filled in his progress and buried him in gravel up to his ankles. "I don't think we can dig ourselves out!"

The nightmares closed in on Amy like circling sharks. What could be worse than being lost in the dark? Being *trapped* in the dark . . . *dying* in the dark . . .

She peered at the shadowy silhouette of her brother's face, trying to bring his green eyes into focus. That's when it hit her. "Dan—I can see you!"

"That's impossi—wait! I see you, too! Just your outline. But—"

"There has to be light coming from somewhere," Amy reasoned. "And where there's light, there's—"

"A way out!" Dan crowed.

It was almost imperceptible—not even enough to illuminate the walls of the passage. But it was definitely there—a dull gray-orange glow.

It was still too dark to see, so their progress was slow. Dan tripped a couple of times as the rock floor grew rougher, and Amy walked into the wall where the tunnel turned unexpectedly.

She barely noticed the collision. Around the corner, the glow was stronger. She could see her brother's silhouette without squinting.

"Jackpot!" Dan exclaimed. The black expanse of floor gave way to a narrow rectangle of radiance. "A secret passage!" He lowered himself into the tight opening. "I'll bet there's a ladder somewhere. . . ."

A yelp was followed by a muffled crash. "Or maybe not," he groaned from below. "Get down here. I think I found something."

Gingerly, Amy eased herself into the tiny space, feeling for footholds in the rock. Soon she discovered what her brother had missed—a series of notches carved into the wall. Dan helped her down into an open chamber lit with oil lamps. After the total blackness of the tunnel, the orange flicker seemed like the arc lights of a stadium.

She looked around. At least half the room was piled to the ceiling with large weathered barrels.

"Could these be a clue?" Dan wondered.

Amy shrugged helplessly. "They won't do us much good if we don't know what's inside them."

The Cahills ventured closer. The drums seemed very old. There were no markings on the oak casings.

"Maybe we can swipe one and roll it out of here." He pressed his shoulder against a cask and pushed with all his might. It wouldn't budge.

Amy came over to lend a hand, and that was when she saw it. An aged desk stood by the wall, half hidden by the stacked containers. On the sloped surface sat a single piece of paper.

The Cahills rushed to examine it. It was closer to parchment than the kind of paper anyone used today—yellowed and brittle. The writing was German, in an old-world calligraphy. It seemed to be a list of some kind, with both words and numbers.

"A formula!" Amy breathed.

Dan frowned. "For what?"

"Our very first clue was an ingredient—iron solute," Amy reminded him. "Maybe this is the whole recipe."

They were silent as the magnitude of her words sank in. This quest was supposed to be a marathon, not a sprint, with clues hidden in every corner of the globe. Was it possible that they had unearthed some kind of ancient "cheat sheet," with all 39 on a single page? Was the contest already won?

Delicately, she picked up the parchment by its edges. "We've got to take this to Nellie. She'll be able to tell us what it says."

Dan let out a whoop. "Can't wait to see the look on the Cobras' faces when we trot out all thirty-nine clues and they're still searching for number two! Or Irina; this time I'm going to hire a real black belt to do the kung fu grip on her. *And* the Holts—hmm, better hire a whole *army* of black belts—"

"We have to get out of here first," his sister reminded him. She surveyed their surroundings. "These big vats came in through a door somewhere. . . ."

"Let's follow the oil lamps," Dan suggested.

The barrel room led to more tunnels. After a few twists and turns, Amy realized they were lost again. She looked down at the flowery German script on the parchment in her hands. The frustration was maddening—to have found their prize against all odds but be unable to bring it to the person who could read it for them.

She consulted her watch. "We're already late for Nellie. Maybe when we don't show up, she'll come looking for us."

"Then I hope she's got one of those giant mining drills," Dan replied, taking note of the sloping floor. Suddenly, he pointed. "Whoa!"

Through an archway in the never-ending passage, they could make out a heavy stone pillar. Propped up against it was—

"A ladder!" Amy breathed.

They rushed over and gazed up through a thick iron grate.

"Sunlight!" she hissed. She had never expected to see it again.

Dan scaled the wooden rungs and pushed at the metal. "Give me a hand, will you?"

Amy joined him on the ladder. Slowly, the two of them were able to budge the heavy grill enough to heave it over. A loud gonging sound resonated. They scrambled through the opening and hoisted themselves into the room.

The large space was lined with small neat cots that rested directly on the stone floor. But that was not its most notable feature. At the foot of every bunk stood a black-robed monk with a shaved crown.

Forty pairs of startled eyes were fixed on the Cahills. Forty mouths dropped open in shock. The Benedictine monks of St. Peter's gawked at the Cahills as if they could not believe such creatures existed.

An older monk, his tonsure ringed with gray, noticed the parchment clutched in Amy's hands.

The cry that issued from him was less than human.

CHAPTER 10

In a body, the Benedictine brothers surged toward her, arms reaching for the precious artifact. Amy stood frozen with fear, but Dan was ready for action. He had already spotted the single small doorway in the dormitory. He wasn't sure where it led, but out of here was good enough.

He grabbed Amy by the arm and began to tow her through the swishing black robes, ducking reaching arms. When it became clear that they were about to escape, the monks' agitation grew. A hand grasped Amy's sleeve, and Dan shouldered it away like a pro football player. Amy leaped over a would-be tackler, and the Cahills fell into a broken-field run for the exit.

Nellie fretted in the Fiat, checking her watch every thirty seconds. Where were they? She should never have let them go into a place where one of their slimy Cahill relatives was prowling around. If that lousy Alistair Oh did anything to hurt Amy and Dan, she was going to feed him his walking stick wrapped in barbed wire.

She turned to the backseat, where the cat lounged, no longer scratching. "They're half an hour late, Saladin. Where can they be?"

And then she spotted them, moving fast through the milling crowd of tourists. Running, even. Looking kind of disheveled — and scared. Her eyes focused beyond the Cahills to the wave of black that was gaining on them. Dozens of robed figures — monks — were chasing Amy and Dan across the abbey grounds.

She started the car and threw open the passenger door. "Get in!"

The parchment thieves did not have to be told twice. They barreled through the gates and piled in, a tangle of arms and legs.

"Get us out of here!" Dan gasped.

Nellie stomped on the gas pedal. The car was already squealing forward as Amy pulled the door shut. Dan stared into the side mirror, watching the enraged monks grow smaller as the car accelerated.

The au pair was bug-eyed. "What happened back there?"

"It's not our fault!" Dan babbled. "Those guys are crazy! They're like mini–Darth Vaders without the mask!"

"They're Benedictine monks!" Nellie exclaimed. "They're men of peace! Most of them are under vows of silence!"

"Yeah, well, not anymore," Dan told her. "They cursed us out pretty good. I don't know the language, but some things you don't have to translate."

"We found a clue," Amy explained breathlessly, "and they didn't want us to take it. I'm positive it's something important!" She thrust the parchment into Nellie's arms. "Can you tell us what it says?"

"Why don't we put some distance between ourselves and the abbey first," the au pair advised, wheeling through the narrow streets of Salzburg. "How'd you like to have to explain to the rental company that their car was trashed by an army of deranged monks?"

Dan was impatient. "We'll buy the rental company and the abbey, too! This time, we scored the big enchilada!"

By skirting downtown, Nellie was able to avoid most of the traffic and get over the bridge quickly. They made a few twists and turns and pulled over on a quiet street. "Okay, let's have a look at this 'clue.'" She picked up the parchment.

"We think it might be some kind of formula," Amy put in excitedly.

Nellie pored over the calligraphy, her eyes widening in amazement. "Oh, my God! I can't believe it!"

Dan grinned. "That good, huh?"

"But what's it the formula *for*?" Amy persisted.

The au pair read the page again and again, as if trying to convince herself that it really was what she knew it to be. "You boneheads! This isn't a clue—it's the recipe for Benedictine!"

"Benedictine?" Amy repeated. "You mean the *drink*?"

Nellie nodded miserably. "It's an ancient recipe known only to the Benedictine brothers for centuries. *That's* why they were chasing you!"

The Cahills were devastated.

"We almost got killed in there," moaned Dan. "And it was all for nothing."

"No wonder the monks were upset," Amy lamented. "It must have seemed like we stole the most important thing they own."

"Well, maybe it isn't a clue," Dan tried to console himself, "but at least that parchment will look cool in my collection."

"Dan!" Amy exploded. "We have to give that back."

"Good luck." Dan was bitter. "If we set foot in that abbey again, those men of peace will rip our heads off."

Amy was adamant. "We can't keep it. Maybe we can mail it to them."

"I can't wait to see the address—third cave on the right, go through fifty tunnels, turn left at the stalagmite. In *German*." He climbed over the seat and joined the cat in the back. "I'm going to sit with somebody who isn't nuts—what's up, Saladin? Hey, he stopped scratching."

"I was going to tell you—before I had to play getaway driver from the Christian brothers. While you were at St. Peter's, I took Saladin to a veterinary clinic."

"Was it fleas?" asked Amy.

Nellie shook her head. "The doctor took off his collar and *this* popped out." She reached into her pocket and produced a miniature electronic device about the size of a thumbnail.

"He figures the corners were digging into the skin. That's what all the scratching was about."

Amy frowned. "But what is it?"

Dan was disgusted. "Don't you ever watch TV? It's a homing device. You plant it on somebody when you want to keep track of where he's going."

Nellie was confused. "Who keeps track of a cat?"

Light dawned on Amy. "Not the cat—*us*! Our competition did this! That's why we can't get ahead in the contest. Wherever we go, someone else always knows about it."

"This has the Cobras written all over it!" Dan growled. "Leave it to a couple of rich kids to buy a high-tech way to cheat because they're too dumb to get the clues on their own."

"Or Irina," Amy reasoned. "This would be kid stuff for the KGB. It could be any of them—even Mr.

McIntyre. Remember — he had Saladin while we were in Paris."

"So what do we do with the transmitter now?" Nellie asked. "Smash it?"

"Drop it down the sewer," Dan suggested. "Let the cheaters go scuba diving for it."

Amy turned serious. "You know, this could be a golden opportunity to put the competition off our scent. We shouldn't waste it on a joke."

Dan scowled. "You never let me have any fun."

"Oh, this'll be fun," his sister assured him. "Listen . . ."

Alistair Oh trudged heavily through the parlors of the Mozart Wohnhaus, putting more weight than usual on his diamond-tipped walking stick. He already knew the location of the next important Clue. Still, while he was here in Salzburg, it made sense to visit the Mozart family's home, just to make sure he hadn't missed anything. One could never be too careful.

But as he made his way through the eighteenth-century musical instruments and furniture, weariness pressed down on him. He wasn't as young as he'd once been, back when he'd made his fortune as the inventor of the microwave burrito. Exciting times — alas, all in the past.

He sat down to rest on a visitors' bench. The money was mostly gone now, and so was his youth. The last thing he needed was a globe-trotting marathon after Grace Cahill's pot of gold. But what a pot of gold: fabulous wealth, limitless power. A return to the glory of his burrito days and beyond.

He'd barely slept at all last night. In truth, his conscience was bothering him over the incident in the tunnel yesterday. No one had told him the small explosive would trigger a cave-in. The plan had been merely to scare Amy and Dan away. Yes, they were adversaries, and adversaries had to be defeated. But he'd never forgive himself if anything terrible happened to Grace's grandchildren.

He'd been up past two A.M. watching TV news. If there had been an accident involving two American children, surely he would have heard about it. Curse Grace and her contest for setting them at each other's throats. . . .

He never finished the thought. Fighting fatigue and lack of sleep, he allowed his eyes to close — just for a moment — and slumped back on the bench, fast asleep.

"Another Mozart house. Oh, joy."

"I didn't pick it," Amy told her brother sharply. "Uncle Alistair did."

Nellie had called every hotel and guesthouse in Salzburg to determine where Alistair was staying.

After two pungent hours hiding behind a dumpster in the alley beside the Hotel Amadeus, Amy and Dan followed their elderly rival to the Mozart Wohnhaus.

Now they lurked in the shadow of a magnificent fortepiano, peering through the antique French doors at the tall figure on the bench.

"Well, there you go," Dan said bitterly. "A million-year-old guy who probably wasn't the life of the party even when he was young. Hey, how come he isn't moving?"

Amy watched as Uncle Alistair's head lolled back on his shoulders, jaw slack, mouth open. "I think he's dead."

Dan goggled. *"Really?"*

"Of course not, stupid! He fell asleep. Maybe we can slip the transmitter into his pocket without waking him up."

"And if he does wake up?" Dan challenged.

Amy pulled the tiny homing device out of her jeans. "We'll have to chance it. Wait here."

Cautiously, she slipped through the doors. It was early, and the museum was not yet crowded. The only other visitors in the room were a young couple with Norwegian flags on their backpacks.

Amy waited for the Norwegians to move on. Her feet barely touching the floor, she approached the slumbering Alistair. Slowly, she reached out with the transmitter. His arm lay across his chest, pressing his blazer closed. There would be no margin for error. . . .

A sound halfway between a snore and a hiccup burst from his throat. Amy froze as he stirred, resettled himself, and went back to sleep.

This isn't going to work. The slightest touch will wake him. . . .

Her eyes fell on the walking stick leaning against the bench by Alistair's knees. She scanned the cane for a nook or cranny where she could plant the chip.

Dan was in the doorway, gesturing with both hands. She regarded him impatiently. *What do you want, dweeb?*

At last, she recognized the twisting motion of his fists. She grasped the head of the cane and turned. To her delight, the tip began to unscrew.

Perfect — the top contained an opening where the diamond had been set. It was just the right size for Amy to insert the transmitter.

She was about to replace the piece when she noticed that the walking stick itself was hollow. Why not just solid wood? Unless . . .

She picked up the bottom of the cane and squinted inside. There was something in there! A paper, tightly rolled to fit in the narrow tube.

This was Alistair's hiding place!

She pinched a corner of the page and drew it out. The document was brittle and brown with age — although not as ancient as the recipe they had taken from the Benedictine monks. Hands trembling, she unfurled it. The printing was not in English. But the name jumped out at her, unmistakable:

WOLFGANG   AMADEUS

MOZART

It was all she recognized, but she knew in a heartbeat that this was what they'd been searching for in the tunnels of St. Peter's Archabbey.

So you beat us to it, she reflected, regarding the dozing form on the bench. *Maybe we underestimated you.*

A gurgle came from Uncle Alistair, and his eyelids fluttered.

Working quickly now, she screwed the cane back together and returned it to its leaning spot against the bench.

Alistair slumbered on, completely unaware that his front-runner position had been stolen right out of his walking stick.

CHAPTER 11

Another vital document; another foreign language.

"It isn't German," Nellie announced.

"No?" Amy was flustered. "I just assumed, because we're in Austria—uh, what is it then?"

Their Salzburg hotel room was small and not very nice. Dan was convinced that the management used low-wattage lightbulbs so that the guests wouldn't notice what a dump they were staying in.

The au pair squinted at the document. "Italian, I think. Not one of my languages."

The Cahills regarded her blankly. This was the first time Nellie had been unable to act as their translator.

"So how do you know it's Italian?" asked Dan.

"Spanish and Italian aren't too different. And this word—*Venezia*. I'm pretty sure that's Venice, which is in Italy."

Amy indicated the date—1770. "Mozart would have been fourteen years old. Don't you remember the museum exhibits? He performed all across

Italy around then. His father took him on tour."

"So this is" — Dan frowned — "an eighteenth-century concert poster, starring Mozart?"

"In Venice," Amy finished. "That's where the next clue must be hidden."

Nellie grinned. "I always wanted to go to Venice. It's supposed to be the romance capital of the world."

"Sweet," put in Dan. "Too bad your date is an Egyptian Mau on a hunger strike."

The au pair sighed. "Better than an eleven-year-old with a big mouth."

The drive to Venice took more than five hours. Sharing the backseat with Saladin, Dan nearly went out of his mind. He wasn't a fan of long car rides to begin with. And the frustration of begging the cat to eat was infuriating and worrisome at the same time. They had so little left of their grandmother. They owed it to Grace to take proper care of her beloved pet.

To add to his discomfort, there was also a long, severe lecture from his sister, reminding him of the grave importance of their quest and how much was at stake. "The wisecracks aren't helping, Dan! You have to grow up and take this more seriously!"

"Seriously?" he echoed. "We're already up to our ears in serious! What we need is to lighten up a little! The next clue could be right in front of your nose, but you don't see it because you're too busy being serious!"

"Cut it out!" Nellie bellowed. "You're going to put us in the ditch! They drive the speed of light on these autostradas!"

"*You* drive the speed of light backing out of the driveway," Dan countered.

"I'm not kidding! As long as I'm babysitting"— she glowered at Dan—"*au pairing* — you two are going to have to get along. I can handle the craziness; I can handle your nut-job relatives; I can even handle you disappearing for hours on end. But not the fighting. Understand? You're on the same team. Act like it."

Silence fell, and the argument was over as abruptly as it had begun. With the peace came a release of the tension of their Salzburg adventure. Nellie could almost feel the siblings rebooting, steeling themselves for the dangers that might lie ahead. They were Cahills, all right. Probably the only two decent human beings in the whole brood.

Finally, they approached Venice and the coast. But before they'd even reached the city limits, traffic on the autostrada slowed to a crawl.

"Aw!" Dan glared at the back of his sister's head in the passenger seat. Amy barely even noticed the slowdown. She was studying the Mozart concert announcement and had been since Austria. "What are you doing? Learning Italian by osmosis?"

She ignored the joke. "There's a name on here I can't figure out. Who's Fidelio Racco?"

"Another musician?" Nellie suggested.

Amy shook her head. "Mozart and his sister were a package deal. I never read anything about a third performer on their tours."

"Well, if it really is a concert poster," Dan mused, "maybe this Racco guy is like a promoter."

His sister thought it over. "It makes sense. Not a promoter like they have today. But back then, visiting musicians gave private shows at rich people's mansions. Maybe Fidelio Racco hosted Mozart and Nannerl. I wonder if we can find out where he lived."

"No problem," Dan said sarcastically. "Just look him up in the 1770 phone book. Piece of cake."

"This is Italy," Nellie reminded him. "It's 'piece of tiramisu' here. Mmm, gotta get some. Our exit," she added, roaring off the highway, past a sign marked VENEZIA, onto a wide boulevard. They pulled up behind a television mobile unit with familiar markings.

Dan pointed. "Check it out — Eurotainment TV. Those are the guys who threw that bash for Jonah Wizard in Vienna."

Suddenly, the Eurotainment van squealed left across two busy lanes and made a sharp turn, tailing a silver stretch limo.

Nellie leaned on the horn and barked, "Maniac!"

"Follow him!" Amy said urgently.

"Why?"

"*Do* it!" she insisted.

The wheel just a blur in her hands, the au pair managed to weave in and out of moving traffic, falling in behind the mobile unit.

"Rock on!" cheered Dan. "Paparazzi chase!"

He was right. The limo was trying to get away from Eurotainment TV. But the van driver refused to be shaken. Behind this high-speed game of cat and mouse rattled the Fiat, passing cars, running lights, and swerving around hapless pedestrians.

"When I talked about seeing Venice, this was *so* not what I had in mind!" complained Nellie, hunched over the dashboard. "I wonder who's in the car — Brad and Angelina? Prince William?"

"Keep going!" urged Amy. "I have a sneaking suspicion I know *exactly* who it is."

It happened in the blink of an eye. The limo was speeding toward a bridge, with the mobile unit in hot pursuit. The car turned on a dime, bounced across the ramp, and accelerated down a side street. The van driver tried to follow, but he was hemmed in by traffic. Eurotainment TV disappeared over the bridge.

"Who do I follow?" Nellie demanded.

"The limo!" chorused Amy and Dan.

The Fiat veered away from the bridge and turned the corner. The stretch was traveling at regular speed now. Its passengers believed the chase was finished. Nellie kept well back.

They continued to tail the limo until it veered onto a ramp, climbing a long causeway that led out over a sunlit lagoon.

"Now what?" asked Nellie.

"Don't lose him!" Amy ordered.

"Wait," said Dan. "I thought we were going to Venice. The sign says" — he squinted — "Tronchetto. Smooth move, Amy. Now we're driving to the wrong town."

"I don't think so," put in Nellie. "Look!"

Before them stretched a magnificent sight. A gleaming skyline of domes and spires rose from the sparkling water.

"Venice," breathed Amy. "Just like in pictures."

Even Dan was impressed. "Pretty cool place," he conceded. "Too bad that's not where we're going."

Nellie piloted them across the long bridge, making sure to keep a couple of cars between the limo and the Fiat at all times. At last, they began to descend toward Tronchetto. But instead of a town, they were approaching a low sprawling island, almost entirely covered with thousands of vehicles.

Dan was mystified. "A parking lot?"

"More like the great-granddaddy of them," Nellie amended.

"But who takes a limo to a parking lot?"

A large billboard loomed up on their right. Amy scanned the many languages, zooming in on the English at last. "I get it — there are no cars allowed in Venice! You have to park here and take a ferry to the city."

Her brother frowned. "Then how do people get around?"

"By boat," Nellie supplied. "Venice is crisscrossed by dozens of canals."

Just before the parking entrance, the limo came to a stop. A uniformed chauffeur emerged and opened the rear door. Out stepped two figures, one slender, the other taller and stocky. They wore baseball caps, pulled low over dark glasses. But there was no mistaking the teenager's hip-hop swagger.

Jonah Wizard — with his father, as always.

"*That* bonehead?" exclaimed Nelly in dismay.

Dan was also confused. "If we've got the paper that says Venice, how did Jonah know to come here?"

Amy could only shake her head.

They watched as the Wizards walked over to join a crowd of people waiting to board a ferry to the city. The chauffeur got back in the limo and drove away.

Nellie's brow furrowed. "The great Mr. Hip-Hop Mogul standing in line with the common peasants? How do you figure that?"

Dan grinned. "I'm starting to dig this 'no cars' thing. It's a great equalizer."

Amy wasn't convinced. "Jonah can afford to buy that ferry and kick everybody else off. If he's taking a public boat, it's because he's trying to slip into town unnoticed. Quick, park the car. Let's see where he's going."

The Tronchetto complex was enormous, so they were half a mile away before they managed to locate an open spot. By then, the ferry had moored at the landing, and the passengers were already starting to board.

"Come on!" Dan scooped up Saladin in his arms and began to run for the terminal. "If we have to grab the next boat, we'll lose Jonah for good!"

"*Mrrp!*" complained the Egyptian Mau, displeased with the rough ride.

The deep-throated bass of a horn rattled Tronchetto, setting off several car alarms. The ferry was ready to set sail.

The three sprinted across the lot, backpacks flailing wildly. Luckily, the passenger queue was long, delaying the departure. Dan flung Saladin onto the gangway just as a uniformed sailor was closing the chain behind the last customer. The cat scampered onto the deck, and the exasperated crewman had no choice but to allow the Cahills and their au pair to board with their pet.

The trip to Venice took barely ten minutes. Amy, Dan, and Nellie kept well away from the Wizards, making themselves small behind a bulkhead. They needn't have worried. Jonah and his father seemed just as determined to keep a low profile. They spent the short ride at the rail, faces downcast at the water. And when the ferry docked in Venice, they were the first passengers off, pushing purposefully through the bustling cobblestone streets.

The Cahills and Nellie followed at a distance.

"Taking public transit *and* walking — both in the same day," Dan marveled. "If Jonah gets any more human, the Pez people are going to stop selling his dispenser."

It was easy to remain unnoticed by the Wizards on the busy main roads. But after a few twists and turns, Jonah and his father started down a deserted alley, lined with tiny shops. Amy pulled Dan and Nellie into the cover of a recessed doorway.

Halfway down the block, the Wizards entered a store.

The Cahills and Nellie waited. Ten minutes. Then twenty.

"What are they doing in there?" Amy wondered.

Dan shrugged. "Maybe when you're rich, shopping takes longer, since you get to buy more stuff."

"Let's take a closer look," Amy decided.

Dan handed Saladin to Nellie, and brother and sister approached the store cautiously.

DISCO VOLANTE blazoned a neon sign with the dancing image of a CD morphing into a flying saucer.

Dan made a face. "A music store? Jonah's the Mr. Wonderful of the record business. Anything he wants to hear they'll beam digitally to the home theater in his mansion. Why would he buy his own CDs?"

Amy edged in front of the glass and peered into Disco Volante. It looked like any music shop back in the US — racks of CDs and old-fashioned vinyl records, posters of artists and album covers, a young, slightly scruffy-looking clerk behind the cash register. And—

She blinked. That was it. The cashier was alone. She checked again, venturing farther out in front of the window until she was right in the middle of it. She searched up and down the aisles and into the sound-proof listening booth in the back. Nobody.

Dan noticed the expression of befuddlement on Amy's face. "What is it? Can you see Jonah and his dad?"

"They're not there."

He joined his sister at the window. "We just saw them walk in!"

Amy shrugged. "I can't explain it, either."

Back at the doorway, they brought Nellie up-to-date on their findings.

The au pair was practical. "His name may be Wizard, but he isn't one. He can't teleport himself out of a CD shop."

"Exactly," Amy agreed. "Either Jonah and his dad are still in there, or they left through a secret door. We have to search that store."

"Yeah, duh," her brother put in. "But how do we do that with a guy at the cash register?"

Amy turned to Nellie. "Can you create a diversion to draw the clerk outside?"

The au pair was wary. "What kind of diversion?"

"You could pretend to be lost," Dan proposed. "The guy comes out to give you directions, and we slip inside."

"That's the most sexist idea I've ever heard," Nellie said harshly. "I'm female, so I have to be clueless. He's male, so he's got a great sense of direction."

"Maybe you're from out of town," Dan suggested. "Wait — you *are* from out of town."

Nellie stashed their bags under a bench and set Saladin on the seat with a stern "You're the watch-cat. Anybody touches those bags, unleash your inner tiger."

The Egyptian Mau surveyed the street uncertainly. *"Mrrp."*

Nellie sighed. "Lucky for us there's no one around. Okay, I'm going in there. Be ready."

The clerk said something to her — probably *May I help you?* She smiled apologetically. "I don't speak Italian."

"Ah — you are American." His accent was heavy, but he seemed eager to please. "I will assist you." He took in her black nail polish and nose ring. "Punk, perhaps, is your enjoyment?"

"More like punk/reggae fusion," Nellie replied thoughtfully. "With a country feel. And operatic vocals."

The clerk stared in perplexity.

Nellie began to tour the aisles, pulling out CDs left and right. "Ah — Arctic Monkeys — that's what I'm talking about. And some Bad Brains — from the eighties. Foo Fighters — I'll need a couple from those guys. And don't forget Linkin Park. . . ."

He watched in awe as she stacked up an enormous armload of music. "There," she finished, slapping *Frank Zappa's Greatest Hits* on top of the pile. "That should do for a start."

"You are a music lover," said the wide-eyed cashier.

"No, I'm a kleptomaniac." And she dashed out the door.

He was so utterly shocked that it took him a moment to run after her.

With a meaningful nod in the direction of the astounded Cahills, she barreled down the cobblestone street with her load.

"*Fermati!*" shouted the cashier, scrambling in breathless pursuit.

Nellie let a few CDs drop and watched with satisfaction over her shoulder as the clerk stopped to pick them up. The trick would be to keep the chase going just long enough for Amy and Dan to search Disco Volante.

Yikes, she reflected suddenly, *I'm starting to think like a Cahill. . . .*

If she was nuts enough to hang around this family, it was only going to get worse.

CHAPTER 12

Amy and Dan scoured the store, hunting for trap-doors under tables, behind shelves, and at the back of closets.

Dan threw aside a curtain to reveal a small office. There was a cluttered desk, a sink with a hot plate and ancient espresso pot, and a tiny bathroom. No way out. He tried to open the window. It was sealed shut with countless coats of paint.

"Dan," called Amy. "Look at this."

She was in the listening booth, a tiny enclosure behind soundproof glass. There was a compact stereo system. Two sets of headphones lay on the bench.

Dan tapped on the walls. Everything was solid. "No secret passages."

Amy frowned at the stack of CDs on the counter. "Don't you think the musical choices are a little odd?"

Dan crouched to read the cases. Green Day, Rage Against the Machine, Eminem, the Red Hot Chili Peppers, and, what was this? *Twilight of Genius: The Later Works of Wolfgang Amadeus Mozart.*

He removed the disc and handed it to Amy, who loaded it into the machine. They set the headphones over their ears. Dan was expecting some kind of secret message, so he was disappointed when a string quartet began to play.

He made a sour face at Amy—he'd had enough Mozart to last a lifetime. He examined the CD case. The usual dumb classical music words—cantata, adagio, cadenza. Amy probably knew what they meant. Or she'd pretend to, just to annoy him.

His eyes moved to the bottom of the list: Adagio KV 617 (1791). There it was again. He pressed the forward button, skipping ahead to the final track.

The floor disappeared beneath their feet, and they were falling, sliding down a metal chute. The sides were mirrored, reflecting their own shock back at them.

Amy pressed both hands against the ramp in a desperate attempt to slow her descent. There was zero traction, even when she tried to dig in with the rubber soles of her sneakers. The surface was flawlessly smooth and slick.

What—? Even in her mind, she was unable to form a complete sentence. She squinted, but only darkness loomed below.

Suddenly, a pair of electronic doors separated before them, and Amy saw the bottom rushing up. There was no avoiding it. She braced for impact—

It didn't come. At the last minute, the slide leveled off and deposited them delicately on a soft cushion made of beanbag material. They hopped to the floor in bewilderment. A hallway stretched before them. Stark white walls were covered with paintings. Muted classical music played in the background.

"Another Mozart house?" whispered Dan.

"Can't be," Amy told him. "Some of these paintings are modern. It looks more like an art museum."

Dan was mystified. "An underground museum where you have to slide down from a CD shop?"

Amy stared at a portrait in an elaborate old frame — a man with part of his face in shadow, a stiff white ruff around his neck. "Dan — I'm pretty sure that's a Rembrandt."

Her brother made a face. "You made me mail back the recipe to those monks. Like you're going to let me collect a million-dollar painting."

"If it's real, try fifty million."

"Ka-ching!" Dan gawked at the artwork that decorated both walls of the corridor. "All this must be worth —" He gulped. "There isn't enough money in the world to buy half this stuff!"

Amy nodded. "But here's the thing. Grace was a Rembrandt fanatic. She had tons of books of his paintings. I've never seen this one before."

"Fake?" Dan suggested.

"I don't think so. The style is perfect. And look —" She led him further down the corridor. "That's definitely a Picasso. But it isn't famous, either. I think this might be a secret gallery of undiscovered masterpieces."

"What would that have to do with Jonah Wizard?" Dan wondered.

The classical music ended, and a well-modulated voice announced, "That was the final movement of the Unfinished Symphony by our own Franz Schubert. You're listening to Radio Janus — all Janus, all the time. Next we have a one-of-a-kind recording of Scott Joplin performing at Harry Houdini's birthday party."

As the bouncy ragtime piano rang out, light dawned on Amy. "Janus! That's one of the four branches of the Cahill family! The Janus, the Tomas, the Ekaterina, and the Lucian!"

"I hate Lucians," Dan hissed. "That's the Cobras' branch. Irina, too — remember when she lured us into that weird command center in Paris?"

"I think," said Amy in a hushed whisper, "that this might be the same kind of place. Only this one's for Janus."

Dan was confused. "Who puts a command center in an art gallery?"

And suddenly, Amy just knew. It was as if a thousand-piece jigsaw puzzle had miraculously assembled itself in a fraction of a second. One moment there was nothing but confusion; the next, a complete picture was spread out before her.

"What if each branch of the family has a special skill?" she exclaimed in a hushed tone. "Remember, the famous Lucians were mostly world leaders, great generals, secret agents, and spies. What do those careers have in common? Strategy, plotting—maybe that's the Lucian talent!"

"Okay, but that still doesn't help us *here*—" All at once, Dan clued in. "So you're saying the Janus are artists?"

She nodded ardently. "People like Mozart, a great musician. And Rembrandt and Picasso—"

"And Jonah Wizard!" Dan added excitedly. "I mean, *I* think he stinks, but he's a big star."

"This is *huge*! Jonah came here for a reason. We have to figure out what he's after and get to it first."

"Aren't you forgetting something?" Dan pointed out. "Jonah's a Janus. He's allowed to be here. But we're not."

"Grace never told us what branch we belong to. It might be Janus. I play piano."

"Face it, Amy. You're lousy at piano. And I can't draw a straight line with a ruler. We're about as artistic as a couple of hockey pucks."

She sighed. "We'll be careful. They don't have to know we're here."

They set out down the hall, passing paintings by masters from Van Gogh to Andy Warhol. The corridor was curved, the floor sloping downward.

"This is weird," Dan wondered. "It's like we're spiraling deeper and deeper underground."

"Maybe that's the shape of the stronghold," Amy suggested. "They didn't have a lot of space, so they designed the place like a corkscrew. If they've got the best artists, they've probably got the best architects, too."

He nodded. "Sell a few fifty-million-dollar paintings and you've got enough cash to build whatever you like. You could hire your own private army—" He looked nervous. "You don't think they've got a private army, do you?"

Amy could only shake her head blankly. With this contest, the only predictable thing was that the Cahill family would continue to be unpredictable.

And you can never underestimate the power of the forces stacked against you.

The corridor widened, and there stood a full-size fighter plane from WWI, with propeller, fixed machine guns, and two levels of wings. It was painted with an Indian head on both sides.

Amy regarded it in confusion. "Maybe some kind of modern art?"

Dan's eyes were wide. "This is no artwork—it's the coolest thing I've ever seen live!"

"A real plane?"

"Not *any* plane—this is the Nieuport Fighter flown by Raoul Lufbery! One of the greatest flying aces of World War One! Only"—he frowned—"I thought Janus are supposed to be artists, not fighter pilots."

"I guess that depends on what you call an artist," Amy mused. She pointed to a display case on the wall where a collection of crossbows and rifles was mounted. "Archery, target shooting, aerial combat. On the PA they were talking about Houdini, who was an *escape* artist."

"Sweet," said Dan. "I'm starting to dig these Janus a little bit."

"Dan — over here!" Amy held open the doors of a chrome elevator beyond a model of an F-15 cockpit.

He rushed to join her and examined the floor directory. "Now where to? Sculpture . . . Movies . . . Strategic Planning? Why would you need strategic planning for an art museum?"

"It's not just a museum, remember?" said Amy. "It's a base of operations for the whole Janus branch to plan strategy."

"Yeah, but strategy for *what*?"

"Well, for starters, clue finding."

"Aw, come on!" Dan protested. "The contest was announced at Grace's funeral. No way could the Janus build a setup like this in two weeks, I don't care how many paintings they sell."

"The *official* contest began at the funeral," Amy amended. "The clues have been around since Mozart's time — maybe even before. I'll bet the branches have always known about the thirty-nine clues. And whatever the prize is — this huge secret — *that's* what they've been fighting about all these centuries."

The steel doors hissed shut and the car started its descent into the guts of the stronghold.

Dan regarded his sister with alarm. "Did you press anything?"

She shook her head anxiously. "Someone must have called the elevator!" Fear gripped her. In a few seconds, the doors were going to reopen, revealing a Janus who might know he was looking at two kids who didn't belong.

Amy dove for the panel, slapping at the buttons willy-nilly, hoping to stop the car before it reached its destination. The elevator came to an abrupt halt. Had she managed to send it to a safe floor?

By the time we know for sure, it'll already be too late. . . .

They heard the voices first — not just one or two but the general hubbub of a crowd.

"People!" Dan hissed. "Get us out of here!"

But the chrome panels were already sweeping apart.

CHAPTER 13

Amy and Dan dove out of the elevator and ducked behind the only available cover—a bronze statue by Rodin. They peeked out through the crook of the figure's arm. This room was larger than the tunnel-like corridors they'd seen so far. Hanging banners depicted prominent Janus throughout history. She gawked at the famous faces: Walt Disney, Beethoven, Mark Twain, Elvis, Dr. Seuss, Charlie Chaplin, Snoop Dogg—the list went on and on.

A crowd of about thirty milled around, focusing not on the banners but on three stages that ringed the space. There was a performance of Japanese Kabuki theater on one. Another featured a group of artists in splattered smocks squirting paint from spray bottles at a canvas on a spinning wheel. On still another, sword fighters in fire-retardant jumpsuits dueled with flaming foils.

Dan appeared at his sister's elbow. "What *planet* is this?"

"It's amazing," she replied in a hoarse whisper. "A whole society celebrating art and creativity. I hope we turn out to be Janus. The problem is how do we get past all these people?"

Dan thought it over. "When you go to a movie, what do you pay attention to, the audience or the screen?"

She frowned. "What are you talking about?"

"Maybe we can melt into the swarm and slip out the other side."

Amy wasn't a fan of crowds even when she was totally welcome. The idea of putting herself in the middle of thirty enemies made her nauseous. On the other hand, it was a plan—their *only* plan. Waiting around was risky, too. It was merely a matter of time before somebody realized they were intruders.

"Let's try it."

They stepped briskly out from behind the statue, not quite running, trying to project an air of belonging. Dan sidled up to the fire-sword audience. Amy joined the throng around the squirt painters, who were removing their latest creation from the wheel— a sunburst of reds and yellows. Her timing was perfect. The spectators burst into a rousing ovation, and she applauded along with them. Nervousness turned to exhilaration. She'd done it! She was one of them! A cheering man clapped her on the shoulder and nearly knocked her over.

She was inching away from the overenthusiastic fan when she saw the sign:

Mozart! Of course the Janus branch would have a section devoted to its most famous musical member.

She caught Dan's eye, inclining her head ever so slightly in the direction of the placard. He nodded. As usual, Mozart would be the key.

With everyone focused on the performances, it was easy for them to sneak out of the atrium and down another art-lined corridor.

They passed a couple of side galleries dedicated to prominent Janus Cahills before reaching a doorway marked MOZART: WOLFGANG, MARIA ANNA, LEOPOLD.

"Who's Leopold?" Dan wanted to know.

"Their father," Amy supplied. "He was a famous musician in his own right. He devoted his life to bringing out his kids' talents—especially Wolfgang's."

The room was smaller, but it could have been in one of the museums they had visited, with elegant eighteenth-century musical instruments and furniture.

"These guys could out-Mozart the Mozart houses," Dan observed, examining a wall that was floor-to-ceiling glass cases displaying handwritten sheet music. He frowned at a thick volume on the bottom shelf. "What's this? Looks like a book by Mozart's dad."

"*Violin Method.* Back in the seventeen hundreds, it was the number one violin textbook in the world." She drew in a sharp breath. "Dan—it's the harpsichord Mozart played when he was three! Think about it: You were still in diapers at that age, and here's this tiny toddler pressing keys, listening for 'notes that like each other.'"

"Maybe Mozart was in diapers, too," her brother said defensively. "Just because you're a genius doesn't mean you can use a chamber pot."

Amy's eyes panned the many objects on exhibit, coming to focus on a glass case in the center of the room. Propped up in the display were three yellowed papers covered with elaborate handwriting.

Very familiar handwriting . . .

"The missing pages! The ones that were torn out of Nannerl's diary!"

Dan appeared at her elbow. "What do they say?"

She regarded him with exasperation. "They're in German, dweeb. We have to get them out of here and show them to Nellie."

"That'll be a neat trick," her brother commented ruefully. He indicated a strange device connected to the display case. A small white porcelain tray was mounted beneath a bright light source. "I've seen pictures of these. It's a retinal scanner. You stick your chin in the holder, and the light reads your eyeball."

Amy digested this. "Maybe our eyeballs will pass. Four branches of the family — there's a one-in-four chance we've got Janus retinas."

"And a three-in-four chance that we're toast. Amy, these guys have zillion-dollar paintings just hanging off nails in the wall, and we're going after the one thing they put under tight security. I don't understand it, but it's pretty clear that if we try to jack those pages and get caught, payback is going to be a monster."

Amy stepped away from the scanner. There was no question that Cahills played for keeps. With ultimate power at stake, did taking a risk mean laying their lives on the line?

Her anxious thoughts were interrupted by a famous voice in the hall outside the Mozart room: "This place is off the hook, yo! Mom never told me all these heavy hitters were Cahills. . . ."

CHAPTER 14

Dan went white to the ears. He turned to his sister and mouthed, "Jonah!"

Amy dragged him behind the Mozart family's harpsichord. There they cowered, barely daring to breathe.

"It *is* impressive," agreed another voice, this one with an Italian accent. "Clearly, the Janus name made a greater contribution to the arts than any family in human history."

"We got it going on," Jonah drawled.

"Here's a piece that will be of special interest to an American," the man told Jonah. "Perhaps the most widely copied picture of all time—the portrait of your first president, George Washington, printed on every US dollar bill for more than a century. Painted by Gilbert Stuart in 1796. His great-grandmother was born Gertrude Cahill."

"Tight," said Jonah. "But I thought that picture was in the Museum of Fine Arts in Boston."

ONE FALSE NOTE

113

The host's voice radiated deep distaste. "That is just the rough draft. Most of the canvas is left blank. This piece is—what do you Americans call it?"

"The real deal?" Jonah suggested.

"*Esattamente*. Most Janus artists reserve their very best for us. Remind me to show you Van Gogh's *finished* 'Starry Night.' The lunar eclipse is spectacular. Now if you'll follow me . . ."

Amy peeked around the side of the harpsichord. She could see Jonah and his father escorted by a tall, thin man with jet-black hair tied in a ponytail. They stopped at the glass case with the missing diary pages.

"This is, I believe, what you came for," Ponytail announced. "From the journal of Maria Anna Mozart."

Amy and Dan exchanged a stricken look. Had they come so far only to watch Jonah Wizard snatch their prize from right under their noses?

Jonah regarded the retinal scanner. "Serious security. These papers must be all that."

The host was apologetic. "In truth, we are not certain why these particular pages are so valuable. But over the centuries, they have been the object of much warring between the branches. It was only prudent to take precautions."

Jonah's father spoke up. "Jonah doesn't do retinal scans. His eyes are insured with Lloyd's of London for eleven million dollars." He tapped his BlackBerry in annoyance. "No signal down here."

"Chill, Pops. One time won't hurt." Jonah placed his chin in the holder and stared into the light. There was a beep, and a computerized voice announced, "*Confirmation complete — Wizard, Jonah; mother: Cora Wizard, member, Janus high council; father: Broderick T. Wizard, non-Cahill, limited Janus authorization.*"

Mr. Wizard scowled. He was obviously not pleased to be a second-class citizen in Janus-land.

Ponytail put on latex gloves and handed a pair to Jonah. Then he slid open a door in the bulletproof glass, removed the Nannerl pages, and presented them to the young celebrity. "You'll review them in our office, of course. Naturally, we can't allow them to leave the stronghold."

"I'm sure my wife will be interested to know how you run this place like an armed camp," Mr. Wizard grumbled, "even for her own son."

"Your wife," the guide sniffed haughtily, "designed our security protocols personally."

"It's fine, Dad," Jonah soothed. "Mom's down with it, and so am I."

The trio left the Mozart room. Amy leaped up to follow, but Dan put an iron grip on her arm.

"What are you going to do?" he hissed. "Mug Jonah Wizard in the middle of Janus headquarters?"

"We can't let him go!" she retorted. "We might as well just hand him the whole contest!"

"Getting yourself caught isn't going to change that!" her brother insisted. "This is *his* turf! We'd have to fight a gang of crazy artists who'd rip our heads off for those three pages because they love these dumb museum pieces more than life itself!"

She looked startled and then determined. "You're right! They'll do anything to protect their artwork! Come on!"

She ran into the hall. Dan followed, confused, but ready for action.

Ahead of them, the Wizards and their host stepped into the atrium, pausing to observe the squirt painters and their spinning wheel. In another moment, they'd be lost in the crowd. It was now or never.

Amy dashed past Jonah, leaped onto the stage, and snatched a tube of liquid red from a bewildered artist.

Jonah pointed. "Hey, isn't that—?"

Before he could finish the question, Amy jumped down again. In a few seconds she'd be the center of attention, but her fear of crowds was the last thing on her mind. Every fiber of her being was focused on what she had to do.

Ponytail turned on her. "Who are you? How did you get in here?"

Amy ran to the legendary portrait of George Washington. "Freeze!" she ordered, pointing the paint at the picture on the wall. "One more step and George gets it!"

Ponytail's eyes widened in horror. "You wouldn't dare!"

"Are you kidding?" piped up Dan. "That's my sister! She's on the edge!"

Jonah slipped the diary pages inside his jacket. "What do you Cahills want?"

"Those papers you're trying to hide," Amy told him. "Hand them over."

"They're nothing!" Jonah babbled, unable to believe that Amy and Dan had outmaneuvered him *here*, in his own branch's stronghold. "Just garbage, yo. I was looking for a trash can—"

"Cough them up, Wizard," Dan snarled.

"Forget it."

Amy brandished the paint tube an inch from the first president's face. "I'm not afraid to use this!"

"You're bluffing!" Jonah accused. But behind his bravado, his confidence was weakening, cracks forming in the legendary Wizard attitude.

"Slime him, sis," Dan urged. "Make him a redcoat."

Amy hesitated, overcome with guilt. This was a priceless painting, an American treasure, and she was going to have to ruin it. Otherwise they were doomed. How could things ever have come to this?

She took a deep breath and steeled herself to do the deed.

"*No-o!*" The cry that came from Ponytail was like an air raid siren. "You can have the pages! Just don't harm that picture!"

Jonah's father was appalled. "You don't have that authority! This place may look like a museum, but it isn't one! You're talking about handing over vital information to the enemy! There's a lot more at stake here than a *painting*!"

"You are not a Janus, sir!" Ponytail stormed. "Your kind will never appreciate the unique and irreplaceable life force in any work of art—let alone a priceless masterpiece!"

"Last chance!" Dan exclaimed.

Jonah hesitated. He understood Ponytail's anguish—the George Washington painting was part of Janus history. But Dad knew that the diary papers—clue hunting, the *contest*—could be its destiny. What was the right call? The president or Nannerl? The past or the future? Nervously, he shifted his weight from side to side, unsure of what to do, unused to being unsure.

Amy's eyes met her brother's. They'd never have a better chance. She swung the paint tube around and emptied it into the faces of Ponytail and the two Wizards. While the three floundered, rubbing red out of stinging eyes, Dan sprang. He wrenched the diary pages from the disabled Jonah, and the Cahills fled down the corridor. The last thing they heard before a deafening alarm went off was the voice of Ponytail assuring the Wizards, "Don't worry. They won't get far."

Amy and Dan pounded through the corridors, spiraling deeper into the guts of the underground complex.

"Shouldn't we be going up, not down?" rasped Dan, tucking the pages in the crook of his arm, football-style.

Amy nodded breathlessly as the wisdom of his words cut through the urgency of their flight. Escape meant finding a way *out* of the stronghold. They were running in the wrong direction.

Then she spotted it. Partially hidden by a modern art installation featuring a tall pyramid of soda cans was a narrow doorway. And through there—

"Stairs!" Amy grabbed her brother's arm. "Let's go!"

"Yo!" Jonah barreled onto the scene, his well-known face stained red. "You'll never make it, you guys! Come back and we can work something out!" His shouts were barely audible over the blare of the Klaxon.

His father appeared at his side, followed by Ponytail and several other Janus. They did not look like they wanted to work something out. Pure, unadulterated rage radiated from them.

The message flashed between the Cahills as if by radar: *Now!*

They hurled themselves into the pyramid, sending an avalanche of soft drink containers pelting down on their pursuers. There were cries of shock and fury as Jonah and the Janus slipped and tripped on thousands of empty cans.

The alarm blasting in their ears, Amy and Dan sprinted up the concrete steps.

"Where are we?" Dan panted as they ran. "Any idea how to get back to the CD shop?"

Amy shook her head helplessly. "There must be a different exit!"

But her heart sank as she swung around the next landing. Twenty feet ahead, at the top of the flight, the stairwell was blocked by an iron barrier.

Dan hurled himself at the gate. "Ow!" He bounced off, rubbing his shoulder.

Amy worked at the padlock. "No use!" she panted. "We'll have to find another way."

They pushed through a heavy curtain, stumbling into the only hallway they'd seen so far that wasn't plastered with art.

Dan wrinkled his nose. "What stinks?"

"Garbage," Amy decided. "Even great artists have to take out the trash. They must get rid of it somehow. There has to be an exit close by."

They were halfway down the corridor when two jumpsuited figures appeared at the far end. Amy and Dan squinted in the dim light at the flames dancing on their dueling swords. One of the squirt painters stepped out beside them.

Oh, no! thought Amy in despair. *The whole stronghold is after us now!*

The Cahills wheeled to backtrack, only to see Ponytail and the Wizards blocking their retreat.

Jonah shook his head, clucking in false sympathy. "Told you guys — no way out."

They were about to be sandwiched between advancing Janus.

"Got any more miracles?" Dan asked through clenched teeth.

Amy didn't answer. She was staring at a lever right smack-dab in the middle of the wall. It didn't seem to be connected to anything. AIR LOCK read the control, with translations in several languages. There were two settings: PUMP ON and PUMP OFF.

She stared. She had no idea what the device was, but one thing was clear: It couldn't possibly make their situation any worse. She heaved the switch to PUMP ON.

And there was her miracle.

CHAPTER 15

A panel of wall swept back to reveal a Plexiglas chamber filled with water. With a loud thrumming noise, the water was sucked away. An airtight hatch hissed open. There was no hesitation. This might be a trap, and a deadly one at that. But with enemies coming at them from both sides, it looked like escape.

Dan in the lead, they scrambled up a metal ladder.

He was mystified. "Where did all this water come from?"

"You're in Venice, dweeb!" Amy's arms and legs worked like pistons. "The canals, remember? Keep climbing!"

"Look—" he exclaimed. "Daylight!"

The late afternoon sun shone down through the grill of a sewer grating. Amy knew a brief moment of panic. Manhole covers were iron and weighed hundreds of pounds. What if they were trapped?

Her fear disappeared as Dan easily flipped the grating aside. "Plastic!" he chortled. He scrambled out of the shaft and pulled his sister up beside him.

They took stock of their surroundings. They were on a narrow stone dock along one of Venice's famous canals.

Dan looked around in amazement. "Whoa—it's like the road is the water! And people drive boats instead of cars!"

Amy nodded. "Some Venetians hardly ever set foot on the street. They can get everywhere they need to go on the canals."

Their tourist moment was cut short when they heard the echo of a shoe on the metal ladder, and Jonah's voice called, "This way!"

They fled down a narrow walkway that joined their dock to another one.

"Whoa!" Dan pulled up short and just in time. The path ended abruptly. He had nearly given himself—and Nannerl Mozart's diary pages—an unexpected bath in dirty canal water.

"What are we going to do?" Amy squeaked.

They watched as a motor launch pulled alongside the small pier they were standing on and tied up to a pylon. A young woman jumped out and ran into the row house that abutted the dock. She was obviously on a quick errand because she left the keys in the ignition and the motor idling.

Amy took in the inspired look on her brother's face. "That's stealing!"

Dan was already stepping into the boat. "It's borrowing, and it's an emergency!" He pulled his sister aboard, steadying the two of them as the small craft pitched under their weight. "Hang on!" he ordered, and brought the throttle forward.

With a deafening roar, the launch churned about eighteen inches from the dock and lurched to a stop, unmuffled engine protesting.

"You forgot to untie the rope!" Amy stooped to release the mooring line, and they plowed into the narrow waterway.

Behind them, the fake manhole cover flipped open again, and out climbed Jonah, his father, and the man with the ponytail. They ran to another dock and jumped into a motorboat. Several Janus were hot on their heels. Two more craft took to the murky waters.

Dan accelerated, steering toward the closest thing the canal had to a passing lane. Slender gondolas bobbed like corks in their wake. Gondoliers shook their fists and cursed.

"Dan, this is crazy!" Amy quavered. "You can't drive a boat!"

"Says who? It's no different from Xbox!"

Wham! The port-side rubber bumper at the launch's bow slammed into the end of an ancient cobblestone wharf. The small craft spun like a top, pitching Amy to the deck. Only an iron grip on the wheel saved Dan from a similar spill.

He hung on for dear life. "Okay, scratch Xbox — think bumper cars! I rock at those! Remember the carnival?"

His sister was on her hands and knees, clinging to the gunwale. *"Forget* the carnival! Get us out of here!"

He followed her gaze. It was the Janus — gaining on them. The Wizards were in the lead, weaving between slow-moving gondolas.

Dan took a tight corner too wide. With a crunch, the launch bounced off a moored skiff and ricocheted into the middle of the canal.

Amy was terrified. "You're going to drown us both!"

"You want me to stop and give the Wizards a chance to do it?" he shot back.

Dead ahead, the passage split off in three directions. The leftmost path was skinny, jagged, and inhospitable. Perhaps the Janus would avoid it.

Dan headed for it. "Am I ever glad those old-time Venice guys put in these canals!"

"I don't think anyone built the canals," Amy panted. "Venice is really a bunch of tiny islands so close together that the space between them forms waterways."

"Yeah, well, they rule. I just wish this dumb boat would go faster."

Amy glanced nervously astern. "Maybe we've lost them."

Her brother was skeptical. "Not for long. Listen, if Jonah catches us, those diary pages had better not be here. We've got to ditch them."

"Ditch them?" Amy echoed. "We nearly got killed breaking them out of the stronghold!"

"That's why we have to stash them in a very safe place. Then we can wait till the heat's off and come back for them."

She was nervous. "We don't know Venice! If we hide those pages, we might never find them again!"

"All the more reason we have to find a place that's impossible to forget."

"Like what?"

"Like *that.*"

They passed under a low street-level bridge by a modest church — Santa Luca. A small pleasure craft was moored there, partially concealed underneath the span. The name was painted on the stern: *Royal Saladin.*

He cut the motor, allowing the launch to glide toward the other boat.

"Too fast —" Amy cried.

The collision rocked both vessels, and Amy was very nearly pitched overboard. She glared at her brother. "Do you have to drive like such a maniac?"

He looked hurt. "I thought I was doing great. Okay, hold us in place, will you?"

Amy grasped the *Royal Saladin*'s safety rail, surprised at how little strength it took to keep them from drifting. Dan hopped aboard and began the search for a hiding spot.

"Make sure it's somewhere dry," Amy instructed. "If the papers get wet, they'll be ruined."

"Got it." The stern was ringed by built-in benches. Dan unzipped a waterproof seat cushion, removed the

Nannerl pages from his jacket, and sealed them inside the vinyl pad.

No sooner had he stepped back aboard the launch than the bray of outboard engines reached their ears. The three Janus boats raced around a bend in the canal. Jonah Wizard stood on the bow of the lead craft like a hip-hop hood ornament, pointing and shouting.

"Let's go!" urged Amy.

Dan heaved on the throttle, and the launch burst forward in a cloud of burnt oil.

The Cahills had a head start, but there was no way they could outrun their faster pursuers. Their one chance was to get lost in the maze of canals. But this was not to be. Just ahead, the tight channel fed into an expansive waterway bustling with marine traffic.

"The Grand Canal," Amy said with awe. "And there's the Ponte di Rialto, one of the most famous bridges in the world."

"We don't need a guided tour! We need a place to disappear!"

The launch lumbered out into the open. Dan looked astern. Jonah and the Janus were a quarter mile back but closing.

Then he spotted it. Among the dozens of boats on the busy waterway, a gleaming high-tech yacht stood just before the Ponte di Rialto. His first assumption was that it had been moored there, but on closer inspection, he saw that it was about fifteen feet from shore, dead in the water, bobbing imperceptibly.

If we can get behind that thing . . .

He pointed the bow at the empty space between yacht and seawall.

Amy clued in. "You think we can hide? We'll never get there in time!"

Dan leaned on the throttle. "We will."

"How can you be sure?"

Dan wasn't sure of anything—just that they were committed to this plan. All they could do was carry it out.

And pray.

CHAPTER 16

Amy's eyes were riveted astern where, she knew, Jonah and the Janus would appear any second now.

At the last possible instant, Dan let up on the gas. The launch floated into the shadow of the yacht just as Jonah's boat burst into the open.

Standing on the bow, the young star surveyed the Grand Canal in both directions. The Cahills were nowhere to be seen.

His father shut his cell phone in disgust. "I've tried all our contacts at the Venice radio stations. Nobody has a traffic copter in the air right now."

"Their craft is slow," put in Ponytail. "They cannot be far."

Jonah nodded. "We'll split up, yo. We'll head under the bridge and check out that direction. Tell the others to go the opposite way."

Ponytail shouted the instructions to their Janus colleagues, and the two boats raced for the bend in the waterway that led to the Bay of San Marco. Then he put their motor in gear and roared through the stone arches beneath the Rialto Bridge.

An eye peered over the gunwale of the launch and watched Jonah and company disappear in the distance.

"They're gone," Amy whispered. "What now?"

Dan popped up beside her. "I don't know. I honestly wasn't expecting this to work."

"Let's get our diary pages and find Nellie," Amy said urgently. "The Janus won't stay away forever."

Dan reignited the motor and piloted the launch out from behind the yacht. "I think I'm getting pretty good. I haven't hit anything for, like, ten minutes."

"That's the *real* miracle."

The thrum of a powerful engine reached their ears, and the water astern of the luxury craft began to churn.

"They're starting up," Amy commented. "Lucky they didn't pull away when the Janus were out there."

As the small craft ventured into the center of the canal, the yacht began to move as well, falling into place behind them. The shadow of her pointed bow towered over them.

Dan leaned on the throttle. "Better speed up. Those guys could run us over and think they've hit a goldfish."

They backtracked along the broad waterway and swerved into the narrower canal that led to the moored *Royal Saladin*, where they'd stashed the Nannerl pages.

"Dan—look!"

The Cahills watched in bewilderment as the high-tech yacht maneuvered expertly into the smaller channel.

"Why would anybody drive a big boat like that into a tiny little trickle?" asked Amy in consternation. "He could get stuck."

"Only one reason," Dan said grimly. "He's following us."

"Why? He isn't one of the Janus."

"Maybe not, but he's right on our tail." Dan had the throttle at maximum, but the yacht was keeping up easily. There was no doubt that the luxury craft could overtake them at will.

The Cahills sailed past the old Church of Santa Luca and under the tiny bridge where the *Royal Saladin* was moored. Amy looked astern in trepidation and was surprised to find the yacht well back, coming to a virtual stop in the water.

"What are they doing?" Dan wondered. "They *had* us!"

It dawned on Amy first. "They're too tall! The upper deck can't make it under the bridge!"

"Yes!" Dan made a rude gesture toward the yacht, which was now reversing up the channel. "In your face, you big doofus!"

"We can't get the diary pages now," Amy warned. "Jonah can't see us, but whoever's on the yacht might."

Dan didn't let up on the gas. "No problem. We'll just lose this guy and loop around to get our stuff." At top speed, he navigated their craft down tributaries far too narrow for a larger boat. "Out of my way, landlubbers! Captain Dan coming through!" The launch lurched as they bounced off a stone dock. "Oops."

"I hope you know where we are," Amy put in nervously.

"Relax." Dan wheeled the launch along another tight channel, and there ahead of them was the Grand Canal. "Once we hit the main drag, it'll be easy to find the right turnoff for the *Royal Saladin*."

The engine groaned in protest, but Dan showed it no mercy. He pushed the throttle as far as it would go, demanding everything the little motor would offer. The wind in his hair added to his exhilaration. In a few more seconds, they would be on the Grand Canal. "Ha!" he cheered. "It takes more than a million-dollar canoe to outsmart a Cahill!"

And suddenly, a wall of shiny metal blocked their way. Where just a second ago the sparkling open waters of the wide channel had beckoned, now the full length of the high-tech yacht moved out into their path.

Desperately, Dan threw the launch into reverse, but there was no stopping. The engine screamed and stalled out. The Cahills continued on an arrow-straight collision course.

Amy heard someone screaming and recognized her own voice. Dan shut his eyes. It was his only option.

The launch rammed into the steel hull and came apart like a balsa wood model.

Everything went dark.

CHAPTER 17

Amy was no longer in Venice.

She stood in a strange underground chamber hewn into the native limestone beneath a church in the Montmartre section of Paris. On the wall before her was a faded mural of four siblings named Cahill. Luke, Thomas, Jane, and Katherine — the ancestors of the family branches, Lucian, Tomas, Janus, and Ekaterina. And in the distance, a burning house. Even then, centuries ago — conflict, violence, tragedy.

We're still at each other's throats — this time over the 39 Clues. What were they fighting about back then?

The image shifted to a different burning building. With a stab of pain, Amy recognized her own childhood home. Her poor parents, trapped inside . . .

Through her anguish, she struggled for logic. *How can I remember this? I wasn't a spectator at that fire! I had to be pulled out of it!*

Amy and Dan had been rescued. Mom and Dad . . .

The blast of grief was too powerful — a gale-force wind that could not be withstood.

Make it stop—

The picture changed to something she recalled all too well. The funeral—dark clouds, dark suits, and dark veils. Tears—so many, and yet not enough, not nearly. Somber faces—four-year-old Dan, too young to comprehend the scope of the heartbreak that had befallen them; Grace, now dead and gone herself; awful Aunt Beatrice; Mr. McIntyre, friend or enemy? It was impossible to be sure. . . .

Far beyond the grave site, indistinct in the ground fog, she could just make out another figure, dressed entirely in black.

Impossible! No way could I remember that!

But their enemy was coming into clearer focus—his gray hair, his sharp eyes. His lips were moving. He was calling to her. What was he saying?

"Amy—"

She awoke with a start. Dan knelt over her, gently shaking her arm. His hair and clothes were wet. Her T-shirt and jeans felt cold and damp, and her toes squished inside clammy socks and sneakers. She ached all over from countless bumps and bruises. Dan's lips were swollen. A gash on his cheek looked raw.

The launch. The *accident* . . .

She sat up on a narrow bunk. "Where are we?" The room was tiny, yet oddly luxurious, with rich dark paneling and shiny brass hardware on built-in drawers and cabinets.

"Shhh," her brother whispered. "I think we're on the yacht."

She got shakily to her feet. The deck pitched slightly. Water lapped below them.

"Door's locked," Dan supplied, seeing her eyes travel to the closed hatch. "I've heard voices outside. I don't think Jonah's one of them, though."

Amy looked nervous. "I've got a bad feeling about this, Dan. What if we escaped from the Janus only to get caught by somebody even worse?"

"Worse?" echoed Dan.

She bit her lip. "Do you think they could be the Madrigals?"

In the search for the 39 Clues, the mysterious Madrigals were the wild card. Amy and Dan had no information about them beyond William McIntyre's dire warning: "Beware the Madrigals." The lawyer had refused to provide any more detail, but his somber face and urgent tone had spoken volumes. There was little question that the group was extraordinarily powerful and possibly deadly.

The hatch was thrown open. "What do *you* know about Madrigals?"

Dark hair, olive skin, handsome features. It always made Amy guilty to find him good-looking. Ian Kabra. His sister, Natalie, stepped into the compartment behind him.

So it wasn't the Madrigals, but this was nearly as bad. Of all the other teams, the Kabras were the most ruthless. Like Irina Spasky, they were Lucians—the cold-blooded and conniving branch of the Cahill family.

Dan stuck out his jaw. "We know more about them than you!"

Natalie rolled her eyes. "Nobody understands the Madrigals. No one's even sure who they are."

"No one except Grace," Dan blustered, "and she told *us*!"

"Liar!" Ian's complexion reddened.

Dan smiled. "Touchy! I guess you don't like it when somebody knows something that you don't."

"Our parents tell us *everything*," Ian said haughtily. "Not like your precious Grace, who left you in the dark and then turned you loose to wreck the contest!"

"Calm down," Natalie said to her brother. "He's just trying to get to you—and succeeding. For someone who's smarter than a supercomputer, sometimes you're a real idiot."

"What do you want?" Amy demanded.

"Only what you stole from the Janus stronghold," Natalie replied reasonably.

"I don't know what you're talking about," Dan said stubbornly.

"Don't play dumb," Ian snapped. "Although you *are* a natural—"

"We know the stronghold exits somewhere in the canal network," his sister interrupted. "We put surveillance cameras all over Venice. But when Jonah turned up chasing *you* — well, it wasn't hard to connect the dots."

"We were in the stronghold," Amy admitted, "but we didn't take anything. It's just an art museum down there."

"Search us if you don't believe it," Dan added.

"As if we hadn't already done that," Natalie said in bored exasperation. "You've lost weight, Amy. I don't think this contest is good for your health."

Amy ignored the barb. "So you know we're telling the truth."

"The two of you make me sick," Ian spat. "You look like you crawled out of a sewer. . . ."

"We *did* crawl out of a sewer!" Dan returned defensively.

"It wouldn't exactly have been a great loss if you hadn't wormed your way out of that tunnel explosion in Salzburg."

"That was *you*!" Amy accused.

Ian snorted. "You think it was hard to fool Alistair into thinking he was our ally? We should have given the old stick insect a bigger bomb. Then we'd be rid of the lot of you."

Natalie sighed. "Forget it, Ian. They have nothing. Captain!" she called sharply.

A burly sailor appeared in the companionway. "Yes, miss?"

"These stowaways need to be put off the ship."

"We didn't stow away!" Dan protested. "You sunk our boat and pulled us out of the canal!"

"Good point," Ian agreed. "Return them to the canal. Roughly, please."

The captain's expression was impassive as he dragged the Cahills topside. He had an iron grip that reminded Dan of his dealings with the Holt family.

Night had fallen, and the lights of Venice surrounded them. They were on the Grand Canal, twenty feet offshore, moving slowly.

"Come on, mister," Dan wheedled. "Give us a break."

The man betrayed no emotion. "I have my orders." And with a single heave, Dan was up and over the rail. He tucked in his knees and hit the water with a cannonball splash. Seconds later, Amy struck the surface a few feet away, flailing and gasping.

Neither had been conscious during the wreck of the launch, so they did not remember the feel of the water. It was freezing cold and jump-started both hearts to jackhammer speed. Fueled by adrenaline, they struggled to the edge and scrambled up the seawall.

Dan shook himself like a wet dog. "Okay, let's get our diary pages."

"We can't." Amy hugged herself to control her shivering. "We're not going to find the thirty-nine clues if we both have hypothermia. We need Nellie and dry clothes."

Dan glared resentfully at the retreating yacht in the distance. "A grenade launcher would be nice, too."

"Never mind the Cobras. The way to get back at them is to win."

"I'm with you there," Dan told her. "But where do we look for Nellie? That music shop feels like a hundred years ago."

"Doesn't matter," Amy said with confidence. "She's loyal. She won't leave without us. Disco Volante it was called. Hope the water-taxi drivers have heard of it."

Dan reached into his soggy pocket. "Hope the water-taxi drivers don't mind wet euros."

Never before had Nellie Gomez been so worried.

She slumped on the wooden bench, squinting into the dim light of the streetlamp in front of Disco Volante. The clerk she had run ragged had closed up and gone home an hour ago, never noticing that she was still there, casing the place.

Where were Amy and Dan? How could two kids go into a music store and never come out?

"*Mrrp,*" was Saladin's comment from her lap.

"That's easy for you to say," Nellie quavered. "You're not in charge of those two maniacs."

It was coming up on four hours now—four hours to ruminate on one simple dilemma: When was it time to call the police?

They had never discussed it because it had always been unthinkable. Police meant discovery, which sooner or later would land the kids in the custody of Massachusetts Social Services. They'd be out of the contest for good. But now it was starting to look as if police meant rescue, which meant saving their lives, regardless of where they ended up.

"Wait here," she told Saladin, as if the cat had a choice. Even Nellie wasn't sure what she was planning to do. Heave a brick through the window, probably, and storm the place. Now she could be arrested in two European cities instead of just one.

As she approached the store, two shadowy figures rounded the corner. She ducked into a doorway, spying on the newcomers as they approached Disco Volante, trudging slowly, wearily. A male and a female, not quite adult size—

When she recognized Amy and Dan, she raced over and swept them into her arms. "You guys—thank God! I was just about to—yuck, why are you all wet?"

"It's a really long story," Amy said wearily. "We've got to get into dry clothes, and then we need to pick something up."

"We'll explain on the way," Dan promised.

They found an alcove that offered a measure of privacy. Amy and Dan were already so deeply chilled that changing clothes in open air was pure agony. But they felt their circulation resuming as they struggled into dry things. Next came the hard part—locating the Church of Santa Luca on foot rather than via the canal system. They wandered for a while before finding a shuttered tourist kiosk with a city map.

"Amazing," marveled Amy as they plotted their course through streets and over bridges. "The founders of Venice took a collection of rocks and turned it into one of the world's great cities."

"I'll be more in the mood for town history when we've got those Nannerl pages in our hands," announced Dan.

Navigating the narrow serpentine streets made them feel like rats in a maze. Several times they could see where they wanted to go but were unable to get there because a canal was in the way. Add to that the fact that the Venice skyline had dozens of domes and steeples, and they were searching in the dark. After more than an hour, they plodded up beside a small stone church.

"This is it," said Dan. "See? There's the bridge in back."

The night was quiet—just the distant noise of motorboats. Leaving Nellie and Saladin on the front steps of the church, they scampered behind the building to the canal.

Amy pointed. "Look!"

An ancient stone staircase led to the water. They rushed down and froze.

There was the dock underneath the bridge.

The *Royal Saladin* was nowhere to be found.

CHAPTER 18

Amy's vacuum-cleaner wheeze threatened to suck her brother in. "Okay," she told herself. "Don't panic—"

"Why not?" he asked bitterly. "If there ever was a time to panic, this is it! What happened to the boat?"

"Aw, Dan," she moaned, "why'd you have to hide the Nannerl pages on something that can pick up and sail away?"

Dan bristled. Anguish, disappointment, and frustration mingled in his stomach, a roiling, toxic brew. "I didn't have a lot of choice, Little Miss Perfect! I was on a motor launch with half the Janus branch chasing me! And what help was I getting from my dear sister? *'Oh—you can't drive a boat!'* That's all I ever hear from you—you *can't*; we *shouldn't*; it's *impossible!* I saved our butts back there!"

"This isn't about butts," Amy pointed out. "It's about clues, and that means the diary pages."

"Which the *Cobras* would have taken off us if I hadn't stashed them on the *Royal Saladin!*" Dan shot back. "You think I'm a stupid baby who's too immature to understand what's at stake! Well, *you're* the one who doesn't get it! A *contest*; a *search*—who's better at that kind of stuff, you or me?"

She scowled at him. "We're not talking about strafing the neighborhood with bottle rockets—"

"You're treating me like a kid again!" he exploded. "Okay—I like bottle rockets! And water balloons! And cherry bombs! I lick batteries! I *experiment*!"

"You're a regular Madame Curie."

"At least I *try* things," he persisted. "It's better than sitting around biting your nails, wondering, *Should I or shouldn't I?*"

His sister sighed miserably. "Fine. I'm sorry. It still doesn't answer the million-dollar question: What happens now?"

He shrugged. He wasn't ready to accept her apology, but there was nothing to be gained by continuing the argument. "We wait. What else can we do? The boat moored here once. Maybe it'll come back."

She spoke the words he'd been dreading—the awful possibility that haunted him. "What if before was a one-time thing? What if we've lost those pages forever?"

Dan had no answer. All at once, the breakneck pace of it caught up with him. Five hours in the Fiat, tailing the limo, Disco Volante, the Janus stronghold, the canal chase, the Cobras.

And now this.

He could have flopped down on the stone walkway and slept for a year. It was a crushing exhaustion that sucked the strength out of every single cell in his body. He felt old at eleven.

Amy must have sensed this, because she put a supportive arm around his shoulders as they headed back to the church to update Nellie on the latest twist.

"We could be waiting a long time," Amy told her. "Maybe you should find a hotel and get a few hours' sleep."

"If you two think I'm leaving you alone for another minute today, then you've been drinking the canal water," the au pair said severely. "Go and wait. I'll be here."

"Mrrp," Saladin added drowsily.

Good old Nellie. The show of support lightened the mood slightly. The thought of someone who would look out for them — someone older, even if only by a handful of years — seemed almost *parental*. It was a mere penlight in a vast void. Yet Amy and Dan Cahill had seen nothing in that darkness for a very long time.

But as they settled in behind the church to wait, the grim reality began to press down on them. If they could not recover the papers encased in the vinyl seat cushion of the *Royal Saladin*, they were at a complete dead end.

They had staked everything on this quest. Washing out would leave them as nothing more than fugitives from Massachusetts Social Services. Homeless orphans, with no past and no future, stranded half a world away from anyone or anything familiar.

The minutes passed like months, as if time itself had been slowed by the black-hole gravity of their situation. They hugged themselves against the clammy dampness of night, chilled further by fear and uncertainty.

Amy took in the lights of Venice, gleaming off the water. "Weird, huh? That so many bad things can happen in such a beautiful place."

Dan was not on her wavelength. "Maybe we should steal another boat. Then at least we can cruise the canals. The *Royal Saladin* must be somewhere." He looked at her intensely. "Giving up is not an option."

"Then how would we know the *Royal Saladin* won't come back a minute after we leave? Here we are and here we stay."

For Dan, it was extra-special torture. Doing *something*—even the wrong thing—was easier to take than sitting around. The first hour was misery. The second was actual physical pain. By the third, they were numb, sunk deep in despair as the city sounds and motorboat noise diminished, leaving only lapping water and distant accordion music.

They had always known that their quest was a long shot. But neither had expected defeat to take this form—an unfortunate choice stashing a few vital pieces of paper in a hiding place that got up and left.

Both sat forward on the stone path. Was the music getting louder?

The lilting melody swelled, and a boat sailed around the bend of the canal, lit up like a Christmas tree. The open stern was packed with revelers, dancing and celebrating wildly.

Amy and Dan felt like celebrating themselves. It was the *Royal Saladin.*

Dan looked on from the shadows. "A party?"

"Not a party," Amy managed. "A *wedding!*"

The bride and groom embraced by the wheelhouse, while flower girls showered them with rose petals. Laughter rang out. Champagne toasts soared. There must have been fifteen people squeezed onto the small craft, including the accordion player, who was balanced precariously on a dive platform.

Dan was intent on the seat pad, where he knew the Nannerl pages were hidden. "Five thousand boats in Venice, and I had to pick the one from the tunnel of love! What are we going to do? This brouhaha could last all night."

"I don't think so. See?"

Two tuxedo-clad men were clumsily attempting to tie the *Royal Saladin* to the bridge dock. It took several tries, and the father of the bride very nearly tumbled over the rail into the canal. Finally, though, they got the craft moored, and the wedding party began to come ashore.

Amy and Dan ducked behind a half wall as the guests climbed the stairs to the Church of Santa Luca. The best man brought up the rear. Before leaving the

Royal Saladin, he seized the bench cushion as his "partner," dancing onto the dock to the accompaniment of the accordionist.

Both Cahills' hearts skipped a beat. It was the pad that contained the precious diary pages.

The others laughed and cheered as the best man waltzed the pad toward the steps.

A thin film of sweat formed on Dan's brow. *What's this clown doing? Is he really stupid enough to take a seat cushion to a wedding?*

At the last moment, the man tossed the pad back aboard the *Royal Saladin* and followed the rest of the guests up the stairs.

Amy and Dan crouched in silence as the wedding party crossed the churchyard and filed into Santa Luca. Even when they heard the heavy door slam shut, they remained still and hidden. After so many reversals of fortune today, they half expected a meteorite to hurtle from the sky and vaporize them if they dared to move.

Finally, Dan stood up. "Come on. Let's get those diary pages before they end up on the honeymoon cruise."

———○——⟨○⟩——○———

Their Venice hotel was cheap, mainly because it had no water view. That had been the Cahills' one condition.

"No more canals," Dan had said firmly. "I hate them."

While Amy and Dan took long showers to warm up and wash away the none-too-clean canal water, Nellie busied herself with the diary pages. It was only three handwritten sheets. But they contained some astounding information.

"You're not going to believe this, you guys," Nellie breathed. "No wonder somebody ripped these pages out. They're all about how worried Nannerl was. She thought Mozart was going crazy."

"Crazy?" echoed Dan. "You mean, like, stand on your head and spit nickels kind of crazy?"

"He was running himself into major debt," Nellie explained, following the flowery German script with her finger. "Spending more money than he earned. But here's the thing—the stuff he was buying was pointless and weird. He was importing rare and expensive ingredients from overseas."

Amy's ears perked up at the word *ingredients*. "Remember *iron solute*? That's an ingredient, too. All this must be mixed up with the thirty-nine clues somehow."

"Mozart was in it up to his ears," Dan agreed. "Just like Ben Franklin."

Nellie turned to a different page. "The diary mentions Franklin, too—right here. Mozart was in communication with him. You know what Nannerl calls him? 'Our American cousin.' And you'll never believe who else was a Cahill—only Marie Antoinette, that's who!"

"We're related to the queen of France!" Amy exclaimed in awe.

"And the Austrian royal family, too," Nellie went on. "That was the connection. She and Mozart met when they were kids. When she married the future King Louis XVI and went to France, she became the go-between for Franklin and Mozart."

Amy was so astounded by this overload of information that she almost missed the faint pencil lines in the margin next to Nannerl's heavy calligraphy. Her surprise was accompanied by a flood of emotion. "Grace wrote this," she said in a watery voice. "I'd know that handwriting anywhere."

Dan stared. "Our grandmother ripped out part of Nannerl's diary?"

"Not necessarily, but these pages were in her hands at some point. She traveled all over the world. She's mixed up in this quest fifty different ways." She squinted at the spidery script beside Marie Antoinette's name and read aloud:

The word that cost her life, minus the music.

Dan sighed in fond annoyance. "That's Grace, all right. Clear as mud."

Nellie was exasperated. "What's the matter with you Cahills? Why does everything have to be a puzzle? Why can't you just come out and say what you mean?"

"Then it wouldn't be the thirty-nine clues," Dan pointed out. "It would be the thirty-nine statements."

Amy looked thoughtful. "The thing Marie Antoinette was most famous for was this: When someone told her the peasants were rioting because there was no bread, she said, 'Let them eat cake.'"

Dan made a face. "You can get famous for *that*?"

Amy rolled her eyes. "Don't you see? There *was* no cake! There was no food at all! It became a symbol for how the rich were totally out of touch with the needs of the poor. Those words helped set off the French Revolution. And that was when Marie Antoinette died by the guillotine."

"Sweet—the guillotine," Dan approved. "Now it's getting interesting."

Nellie raised an eyebrow. "So you're saying that the word that cost her life was—cake?"

"Minus the music," added Amy. "What could that mean?"

"Well," mused Nellie, "Marie Antoinette spoke French, so—"

"Wait a minute!" Amy exclaimed. "I know this! Grace told me about it when I was a little kid!"

"How come you can always dredge up some weird Grace conversation from a million years ago?" Dan demanded, his emotions suddenly close to the surface.

"She's only been gone a few weeks and I can barely remember her voice."

"That old stuff is important," Amy insisted. "We knew her as a cool grandmother. But all those years, I think she had a hidden agenda, too. She was *training* us for this contest — planting pieces of information that we were going to need. This might be one of them."

"And what exactly is 'this'?" Nellie prompted.

"When Marie Antoinette said, 'Let them eat cake,' she's usually quoted using the French word *brioche*. But Grace was very careful to tell me that she used the more common term for cake — *gateau*."

Dan's brow furrowed. "Cake is cake. Isn't it?"

"Unless this had nothing to do with cake," Nellie suggested. "According to Nannerl, Marie Antoinette was sending secret messages between Franklin and Mozart. Maybe it's some kind of code."

"So *gateau* is a message, and *brioche* isn't — and they mean the same thing?" Dan put in dubiously.

Amy shook her head. "I don't know what it means, but I'm positive it's a piece of the puzzle."

Dan was studying the Nannerl pages over Nellie's shoulder. "There's another note — look!"

The pencil lines were even fainter, but there was no question it was Grace's writing. This time it was right in the center of the page.

$$D > HIC$$

Dan frowned. "Maybe she had the hiccups?"

"Wait—the markings are right over a name." Amy squinted at the page. "Fidelio Racco."

"That's the guy on Uncle Alistair's paper!" Dan said excitedly. "Mozart performed at that guy's house!"

Nellie translated from the German. "It says here he was a big-time merchant and business honcho. Mozart hired him to import some super-expensive kind of steel that was only forged in the Far East. Nannerl blames Racco for overcharging her brother and landing him in debt. And guess what she calls him."

"Blood-sucking money-grubber?" Dan suggested.

"She calls him 'cousin.'"

Dan's eyes widened. *"Another* Cahill?"

Amy unzipped her brother's backpack and took out his laptop computer. "Let's see what we can learn about our Italian relative."

CHAPTER 19

As rich Cahill superstars went, Fidelio Racco was definitely on the B-list. Maybe even the D-list. Google had heard of him, but a search for his surname placed him below Racco Auto Body in Toronto and Trattoria Racco in Florence, and only slightly ahead of the Rack O'Lamb Irish Chop House in Des Moines. The multimillionaire merchant might have been hot stuff in the eighteenth century, but the composer he had driven to the poorhouse had fared much better in the eyes of history.

Although he was no Mozart, Racco's great wealth had founded Collezione di Racco, a private exhibit displaying the treasures and artwork Racco collected during his world travels. It was there that Amy and Dan decided to continue their search the next afternoon, leaving Nellie at the hotel with Saladin and several varieties of Italian cat food. Maybe the change of country would lead to a change of fortune in ending the hunger strike.

The exhibit was located in Racco's eighteenth-century home, which rubbed Dan the wrong way right from the start.

"Racco house, Mozart house," he grumbled as they marched along the cobblestone streets. "Boring house would be more like it."

Amy was losing patience. "Why do you always have to say that? Boring this, boring that! If this house gives us the next clue, it's the most un-boring place on the planet."

"Amen to that," Dan agreed. "Bring it on, the sooner the better."

"We're getting close," Amy promised. "I can smell it."

Dan wrinkled his nose. "All I smell is canal water. Man, I might never get it out of my nasal passages."

Venice really was a great pedestrian city, if you knew where you were going, Amy reflected. The walk to Collezione di Racco was only twenty minutes. That modest distance brought them from their shabby hotel to a large stone mansion in what was obviously a very expensive part of town.

"I guess the ripping-off-Mozart business paid pretty well," Dan commented.

"It wasn't just the money he made from Mozart," Amy explained. "The guy was a major player in international trade. He had fleets of ships all over the globe."

Dan nodded. "Our old-time cousins were such big shots. What happened to all the loser Cahills? You know, regular Joes like us who never got rich and famous."

At the front entrance, they were greeted by a statue of Fidelio Racco himself. If the likeness was life-size, the millionaire merchant had been very short—only an inch or two taller than Dan. Most surprising of all, though, Racco was strumming a mandolin, and his open mouth seemed to imply he was singing.

Dan's eyes narrowed. "Another Janus?"

His sister nodded. "That would explain why Mozart came to him to import that special steel. He figured he'd be safe with someone from his own branch."

"Bad move, Wolfgang," Dan said sagely. "Never trust a Cahill."

They entered the mansion and paid the hefty admission fee of twenty euros. Even now, centuries after his death, Fidelio Racco was still overcharging people.

They toured the exhibit's various rooms, which housed most of the riches of the eighteenth-century world—silk, heavy brocades, and pottery from the orient; silver and gold from the Americas; diamonds, ivory, and spectacular wood carvings from Africa; and exquisitely woven carpets from Arabia and Persia.

"This stuff is amazing," Amy whispered to Dan. "Only a Janus could have such incredible taste!"

The decorative arts were dizzyingly impressive, but the information display explained that most of Racco's great wealth had come from less glamorous commodities—teas, spices, and a rare Japanese steel alloyed with wolfram, which had the highest melting point of any metal.

"For sure that's the steel Racco was selling to Mozart," Amy said positively.

"Wolfram," Dan mused, a far-off look in his eye. "I've heard of that from somewhere."

Amy was skeptical. "Are you sure you're not thinking of Wolf*gang*?"

"No, wolfram. Grace told me about it." He rounded on his sister. "You're not the only grandchild she told stuff to, you know."

Amy sighed. "All right, what did she say?"

He looked stricken. "I was sort of tuning her out."

"That's why she told most of it to *me*—because she knew you'd forget it all."

They wandered through a hallway of exquisite carved and gilt furniture from all corners of the world, which dead-ended in a round room. At the center, bathed in blue light, stood a polished mahogany harpsichord.

"I'm out of here," said Dan. "This is starting to look a lot like you-know-who."

Amy put a grip on his arm strong enough to splinter bone. "It *is* you-know-who! It says right here—this is the instrument Mozart played at his performance in Racco's house in 1770!"

"There's only one problem: It's a harpsichord. It doesn't tell us what D > HIC means. And it has nothing to do with cake, in French or any other language."

"Still," Amy insisted. "Everything we've been through has been leading us to this instrument. It's going to give us the next clue. I'm sure of it."

Dan reached into the pocket of his jeans and pulled out a wadded, crumpled napkin. "Good thing I wasn't wearing these pants when we went into the canal."

Amy was confused. "What's that?"

He unfolded the napkin to reveal the train logo. "The only thing to do with a harpsichord is play music. *This* is music." He turned it over, and there was the version of KV 617 he had reproduced on the train.

Amy had to keep herself from cheering. "Dan, you're a genius! We take a musical clue from Ben Franklin and play it on Mozart's instrument!"

They looked around. The harpsichord was cordoned off by velvet ropes. A uniformed security guard was stationed by the door.

"Well, we can't do it now," Dan observed. "That guy would beat our heads in if we laid a finger on his precious keyboard."

"Good point," Amy agreed.

"The house closes at five," Dan said. "We're going to have to hide out till then."

The art deco bathroom was old, probably from the 1920s or 1930s, with black and white tiles and immaculate porcelain fixtures.

How can you obsess on tiles and toilets at a time like this?
Amy admonished herself.

Well, that was the point, wasn't it? If she worried about the *real* stuff, she'd be a puddle. What if the mansion had an alarm? Or an army of night watchmen? What did D > HIC mean? How could you subtract music from the French word *gateau*?

Too much for a fourteen-year-old brain.

And those were just the crises of the minute. This *family*! To find out you were related to Ben Franklin and Mozart and Marie Antoinette —

There's no describing it! You feel like you were born with royal blood! Like you're a part of history!

But those great Cahills of the past were exactly that — history. They were long dead and buried. Who were the Cahills of today? Jonah. The Holts. Uncle Alistair. The Kabras. Irina. Double-crossers, thugs, con artists, and thieves. People who smiled and called you cousin while reaching around to put the knife between your shoulder blades.

This contest was supposed to be so high and mighty — a chance to shape the future. But the nitty-gritty was more like a reality TV show called *Who Wants to Be a Backstabber?* It was getting more cutthroat by the hour. Were all Cahills so awful? She couldn't picture Mozart in a boat chase or setting off a bomb in a tunnel. How deep did this ruthlessness go?

The fire that killed Mom and Dad was ruled accidental. Uncle Alistair says he knows "the truth." Does that mean it wasn't an accident?

Just the thought of it took all the fight out of Amy. Words like *contest* and *prize* made this whole business out to be some kind of game, but the tragedy of seven years ago was no game. It had robbed her of the parents she loved. It had robbed Dan even of the *memory* of parents. The faintest notion that the fire might have been deliberate—

She felt suddenly, unexpectedly spent. *Maybe we should just give up. Go home to Boston, let Nellie off the hook. Surrender to Social Services; see if Aunt Beatrice will take us back . . .*

And yet she knew in her gut that quitting was the last thing they would do. The last thing they *could* do. Not with the next clue so close. They had no proof that their parents' death had anything to do with the Cahills. But even if it had—*especially* if it had—then it was fifty times as important to win the contest.

She resettled herself on the toilet seat cover and tried to relax. Across the hall, in the men's room, she knew Dan was doing the same. Or maybe he was too dumb to be scared.

No, not dumb. Her brother was smart. Brilliant, even, in his short-attention-span kind of way. He was the one who had come up with this scheme to hide in the bathrooms until the exhibit closed. She'd just been following his lead when they'd ranged through the wings of the old house, taking careful note of the location of the security people. And when one of the guards had begun regarding them with suspicion, it had been Dan's reliable instinct to melt away into another exhibit.

I would probably still be there, babbling lame excuses.

Dan needed her, yet she needed him, too. Like it or not, they were a team — the crazy dweeb and his stammering sister. Not exactly a recipe for world domination.

The butterflies in Amy's stomach threatened to fly away with her. Dan had his talents, but he wasn't exactly a deep thinker about what could go wrong. Amy envied him that. Sometimes she thought about nothing but. She was the Albert Einstein of worst case scenarios.

She checked her waterlogged but still functioning watch. It had been half an hour since the announcement — in six languages — that Collezione di Racco was now closed.

There was the click of a timer, and the bathroom was plunged into sudden darkness. Oh, no! They had no flashlight. How would they get to the harpsichord now?

Carefully, she felt her way past the stall door, straining to conjure up a mental picture of the layout of the ladies' room. She had to find Dan, but first she had to make it out of here!

The sound of footsteps froze her heart. A security guard! They would be caught, arrested, shipped back to the States —

"Amy?"

"Dan, you dweeb! You nearly put me into cardiac arrest!"

"The coast is clear. Let's go."

"In the pitch-black?" she demanded.

Dan laughed in her face. "It's only dark in the bathrooms. The rest of the place is okay."

"Oh." Embarrassed, she followed his voice out through the heavy door. Dan was right. Collezione di Racco was in night mode, with the exhibit spotlights off but every fourth fluorescent bulb illuminated. "Any sign of a night watchman?" she whispered.

"I didn't see anybody, but it's a big house. Maybe he's over guarding the gold and diamonds. I would be. Who steals a harpsichord?"

They hurried through the grand halls, grateful that their sneakers made little sound on the marble floors. The blue light had been turned off, but even in semi-darkness, Amy could make out the ivory glint of the keyboard that had been played by their distant cousin, the young Mozart, in 1770. Excitement surged through her body like an electric pulse. The next clue was close, very close.

And then the cold muzzle of a dart gun at the back of her neck erased all other brain activity.

CHAPTER 20

"We have got to stop meeting like this," purred Natalie Kabra behind her.

Enraged, Dan made a run at Natalie. But Ian stepped from the shadows and grabbed him firmly around the midsection. "Not so fast, Danny Boy. I see you've recovered from your evening swim." He sniffed Dan's hair. "Well, not completely."

"What do you want?" Dan challenged.

Ian regarded him pityingly. "Are you kidding? Like it's a coincidence we're all here. Basically, it's like this: You're going to stand in front of my sister's dart gun while I entertain you with some music."

Roughly, he thrust Dan against the wall and shoved Amy over beside him.

Natalie faced them, holding them at gunpoint. "Don't worry," she promised with mock sweetness. "The dart won't kill you. But you'll wake up in a few hours with a *nasty* headache."

"Again," added her brother. He stepped over the velvet rope and seated himself at the harpsichord, cracking his knuckles with a flourish.

"You're bluffing!" Dan accused. "You don't even know what to play!"

"I'm sure something will come to me," Ian said cheerfully. "Perhaps 'Three Blind Mice.' Or 'Pop Goes the Weasel.' Or maybe a little tune called KV 617."

"How could you know about that?" Amy blurted.

"You think you're so clever, but really, you're pathetic," Natalie scoffed. "We've been following you since the train station in Vienna. We've intercepted your computer's wireless signal. You downloaded this piece from the web, and we downloaded it from you."

"I took the liberty of printing my own copy," Ian added, unfolding a page of sheet music and propping it in front of him.

Amy and Dan exchanged a meaningful look. Ian and Natalie had no way of knowing that the Internet version of KV 617 was not the same as the Ben Franklin clue. Maybe all was not yet lost.

Ian began to play. The metallic sound of the harpsichord reverberated through the tomblike room. It was much louder than Amy expected, and only a little out of tune. What a magnificent instrument! She craned her neck to watch Ian's long fingers dancing across the ivory keys. That was when she saw it—a tiny wire extending from underneath D above high C and disappearing into the burnished wood of the harpsichord.

D above high C. Amy frowned. Why did that sound so familiar?

And then a picture of it formed in her mind: D > HIC.

Grace's note on the Nannerl pages! It's a warning! That D key is booby-trapped!

The notion had barely crossed her mind when she heard the pitch of the music rise and saw Ian's right hand fluttering in the direction of the fateful D.

Her reaction was so natural, so instantaneous, that she had no time to think about how foolish it was. With a cry of *"Don't!"* she leaped forward, bowling over Natalie. The gun discharged, but the dart missed and buried itself in the drapery. Amy was in full flight, determined to knock Ian off the stool before disaster struck. She was a split second too late.

She plowed into Ian just as his finger caressed the booby-trapped key.

BOOM!

With a flash of flame, Mozart's harpsichord blew apart, tossing Amy and Ian ten feet clear. Amy tucked and rolled, emerging unhurt. Ian's head struck the marble floor. He lay there, out cold.

Natalie scrambled to her feet and reached for the dart gun, but Dan was too quick for her. He snatched up the dart from the drapery behind him and flung it like a spear at his adversary. The point buried itself in her shoulder. She raised the weapon, woozily fighting the effects of the knockout formula. Dan braced for impact, knowing the next dart was coming for him. And then Natalie's eyes rolled back in her head, and she dropped like a stone beside her brother.

Dan ran to his sister. "Are you okay?"

Amy crawled to the wreckage of the instrument. The woodwork was in smoldering pieces, but amazingly, the keyboard was intact. Both could now see a second set of wires, which disappeared into the floor.

"Quick! The music!"

Dan stared at her. "It's not going to play *now*. It's on fire."

"Give it here!" She unfolded the napkin and began to press the keys. There was no sound except for a soft clicking. But she "played" on, following the notes exactly from the Ben Franklin clue.

Suddenly, the floor began to shake beneath their feet.

"Way to go, Amy!" cried Dan. "Now the whole building's coming down!"

A section of marble one yard square dropped away on a hidden hinge. The Cahills crouched over the new opening it created. Before them, on a bed of black velvet, lay a pair of gleaming swords.

"Samurai!" Dan said with reverence. He reached down, took hold of a golden hilt, and then stood up and brandished the weapon. "Samurai warriors carried two blades—one short and one long. These must be the short ones. *Seriously* cool."

Amy drew out the other sword and examined the Japanese characters engraved in the metalwork. "I'll bet these are made with that special steel Mozart was interested in."

Dan nodded. "But how can that be our clue? It has nothing to do with the stuff Grace wrote in those diary pages."

"D above high C turned out to be the booby-trapped harpsichord key," Amy explained. "And *gateau* minus the music—" It came together in her mind. "Musical notes are also *letters*, remember? A, B, C, D, E, F, and G. If you take those out of the word *gateau*, you're left with . . . T-U." She looked puzzled. "It doesn't make sense."

"Yes, it does!" Dan exploded. "It's the old chemical symbol for tungsten! *That*'s the thing Grace told me that I forgot! Wolfram is what they used to call tungsten!"

Amy's eyes sparkled with discovery. "That's why Marie Antoinette said 'Let them eat cake.' She wasn't talking about the poor—*gateau* was the coded message between Franklin and Mozart telling him what ingredient he needed. We've got it! The first clue was iron solute; this one's tungsten! That's what this contest is all about! We're putting together some kind of formula!"

It was a supercharged instant—the smoke from the explosion, the steel of the swords, the thrill of a breakthrough. Yet for Amy, there was so much more. This clue brought them closer to winning the contest—

And closer to understanding who we really are!

Somehow, she knew their parents were smiling down on them.

She reached for her brother's hand. The two spent so much time bickering, but this was *their* moment.

We're still in this thing!

Suddenly, the lights blazed on, and a uniformed night watchman galloped frantically into the room, bellowing in Italian. Shocked, Dan wheeled to face him, not realizing he was still holding the samurai sword two-fisted, like a baseball bat, ready to swing. With a terrified yelp, the guard turned tail and ran the other way.

"Let's get out of here," Amy decided urgently.

"What about them?" Dan indicated the Kabras, out cold on the floor.

"That guard will be back with the police any minute. They'll call a doctor."

Hugging their swords, the Cahills sprinted for the exit.

Nellie was ready to throw in the towel.

She could no longer bear the sight of Saladin, gaunt and languid, barely able to work up a decent *"mrrp."* As soon as Amy and Dan got back, she was going to find a fish market and buy fresh snapper. Okay, it was total surrender, not to mention a waste of thirty bucks a pound. But that was preferable to a dead cat.

Grace Cahill may have been a great woman, but as a pet owner, she hadn't known much about tough love.

Nellie frowned at her watch. It was after seven. All the museums had closed a couple of hours ago. Amy and Dan were late again. She was afraid to think about what that might mean.

With a sigh, she decided to give it one more try. She popped open yet another tin of cat food and brought it to Saladin, who was draped over the arm of the couch, listlessly watching *Home Improvement* dubbed in Italian.

"All right, Saladin, you win. You've proven you're the better man. But I can't get you the good stuff until later, so why don't you take a few bites of this to tide you over until the kids get back?" She took a morsel on her finger and applied it to the Mau's tongue during a yawn.

If a cat could look startled, Saladin did. He smacked his palate like a wine taster. Then he lunged for Nellie's finger and licked it clean.

Encouraged, the au pair held up the tin. It was empty in thirty seconds.

"Good boy!" Nellie cheered. "I knew you'd love it if you just gave it a chance! It's cat food—it's for people like you!"

Saladin was halfway through tin number two when Amy and Dan came bursting in the door.

Nellie was beside herself with triumph. "Congratulate me, you guys! The hunger strike is over —" She took in the sight of Dan waving the lethal samurai sword around the tight hotel room. "Put that thing down before you slice your own ears off!"

Dan ignored the warning, but Saladin stopped feasting and ducked under the bed.

Pink with excitement, Amy waved the other sword. "It's okay! It's the next clue!"

"Swords?"

"Tungsten! That's what the steel's alloyed with!"

"Start packing!" Dan crowed. "We're going to Tokyo! Oh, yeah, and way to go, Saladin. We knew you could do it."

A nervous *"Mrrp!"* came from behind the bed skirt.

Nellie was totally confused. "But why Tokyo?"

"That's where the swords are from," Amy explained breathlessly. "That's where the steel was forged. And the exhibit said that Fidelio Racco went off to Japan and was never heard from again!"

"And we have to do it, too?" the au pair demanded.

"The trail leads there," Amy insisted. "That's where we'll find the next clue."

It was the best thing about loyal Nellie Gomez. Without another word of protest, she picked up the phone and called Japan Airlines.

The Kabras had money; the Holts had muscle; Irina had guile and training; Alistair had experience; and Jonah had fame. Amy and Dan Cahill had their wits and little else. Yet only they had uncovered the second clue.

On with the chase.

CHAPTER 21

To the citizens of Salzburg, Austria, William McIntyre looked like just another tourist. More formally dressed, perhaps, in a dark business suit, but a foreign visitor strolling through the public square. Nobody seemed to notice the tiny handheld monitor, nor did they hear the soft beeps emitted by the device as it homed in on the transmitter beacon.

For nearly a week, Mr. McIntyre had used this equipment to keep tabs on Amy and Dan as they traveled from Paris to Vienna and on to Salzburg. But now the signal had stopped moving. In fact, it had not budged in two days. Something was wrong.

As he crossed the crowded plaza, the beeps consolidated into a continuous tone, which meant the transmitter was very, very close.

McIntyre stared. There it was, affixed as a lapel pin to the statue of Mozart in the center of the square.

A strong hand on his shoulder spun him around. It was Alistair Oh, in a towering rage.

"So it's *you!*" the elderly man accused. "I don't appreciate your meddling in this contest! Where is my clue?"

The lawyer shrugged, bewildered. "I have nothing of yours."

"There was a clue from the tunnel at St. Peter's," Alistair said coldly. "When I went to retrieve it to have it translated, I found it missing and *your* homing pin in the head of my cane. Your explanation, if you please."

"I have none."

"So you confess that you're trying to influence this contest." His eyes narrowed. "Or perhaps your plan is to hijack it entirely and take the prize for yourself."

McIntyre rose to his full height. "I resent that. You may well have been bamboozled, but not by me. You ought to know that, with the stakes this high, treachery is to be expected. And Cahills are capable of almost anything."

"You haven't heard the last of this. When I win the contest, I'll see to it that you never work again!" Alistair spun on his heel and stalked away.

With a sigh, McIntyre retrieved the homing pin from Mozart's lapel — it had been affixed with chewing gum. Pocketing it, he exited the square and walked three blocks to an outdoor café in a secluded courtyard. He seated himself at a quiet table, across from a man dressed entirely in black.

"You won't believe it," the lawyer announced in a despairing tone. "They found the homing device under the cat's collar and planted it on Alistair Oh."

The man in black stroked his furrowed brow. "So what you're saying is we've lost the children."

McIntyre nodded glumly. "It's more like the children have lost us. It's possible that they are more resourceful than even Madame Grace had imagined."

High above their table, the vapor trail of a jetliner left a white ribbon in the clear blue sky, heading east.

TOP SECRET

Memorandum

To: Agents with Top Secret Security Clearance

Re: The Cahill Family

ATTENTION! Our spies across the globe report new activity in the Cahill family. Rumors are coming thick and fast. But the best intelligence we have suggests that Grace Cahill (internal codename: Wildcat) has launched a hunt for some sort of "Clues" hidden around the world. Cahills who find "Clues" are eligible for the chance to win $100,000 in prizes.

OUR MISSION: To try to infiltrate the notorious Cahill family and find the hidden "Clues" — whatever they may be.

OUR METHOD: To impersonate actual Cahill family members.

HOW TO HUNT CLUES:

1. Go to www.the39clues.com
2. Click on "Create an Account" and choose a username and password.
3. Discover if you belong to a branch of the Cahill family.
4. Explore the Cahill world and track down "Clues."

Make sure Klose doesn't see thi

Good luck. You're going to need it.